Nandra Hoffman

the ARTISAN way

Nandra Hoffman

Nandra Publishing, LLC
Orlando, FL

Library of Congress Control Number: 2020924416

ISBN-13: 978-1-950697-08-3 (Ebook)

ISBN-13: 978-1-950697-09-0 (Paperback)

ISBN-13: 978-1-950697-10-6 (Hardcover)

Nandra Publishing, LLC

Orlando, FL

www.nandrapublishing.com

Front cover and book design by Nandra Publishing, LLC.

"To every person struggling to find love within themselves."

Prologue

Lyah

Nothing would ever change.

"I expect so much better from you, Aalyah! Why can't you be like Brooke's daughter Keisha? She's going places!" Her mother paced around the living room, her eyes bright with anger.

Lyah would've been more hurt hearing those words coming from her mother's mouth if she hadn't heard them a million times before. Now, it was like a broken record that ceased to end except with a new person to compare her apparent failing life.

She was quite used to her mother commenting on her inadequacies since her father had left when she was nine. Her mother, never one to hold back her tongue, somehow needed a new ear to brutalize once her father was no longer around to take the beating. Naturally, Lyah was the next target considering she had no older or younger siblings. But by now, at seventeen, she couldn't care less what her mother had to say. She blamed her mother for her father's departure, and because of that, Lyah couldn't ever see herself caring for her failing mother like she once did.

Lyah rolled her eyes and sighed. She needed to escape. And fast. Her anxiety was starting to kick in, and that wouldn't be good for anyone.

"Well, why don't you adopt the bitch, then?" She almost wanted to smirk at the flare of rage that sparked her mother's eyes. But she knew better. She hated that.

"You watch your goddamn tongue, Aalyah! I have no time for sass nor your lack of manners!" Her mother stood in front of the chair Lyah sat on, looking like she was about to blow.

"You act like we don't argue over the same thing every week. Every. Single. Week! What more do you want from me? I'm not your golden child. I can't live the dreams you never got to fulfill. It'll never be, and I'm not your pawn!" Lyah yelled.

Though she was quite used to it by now, Lyah couldn't help but defend herself. She had accepted long ago that she was never going to live up to her family's expectations. It's not like they had ever given her the chance to do so anyway. They were already counting her out by the time she hit nine-years-old. She didn't feel the need to try anymore. Unfortunately, that had caused even more of a separation between them and herself. Her father, who was too busy playing house with his new family, barely cared she existed. She cried herself to sleep many nights as a child, wondering why he felt the need to find a better daughter or couldn't just take her with him. Rarely showing his face or calling, he often felt like a distant memory. Her stepsiblings had everything they could ask for and did nothing but look down on her even as kids.

Eventually, Lyah stopped shedding tears over the matter. Nothing ever changed. Nothing was ever going to change. The only thing she could do was accept her place and get the hell out of dodge as fast as she could. Sitting right in front of her hot-headed mother, she couldn't get out soon enough.

"Are you even listening to me? See, this is what I'm talking about, Lyah! You can't even sit through two seconds of constructive criticism without losing focus!"

Constructive criticism? Is that what she called it?

Verbal abuse was a better term. But of course, Lyah's mother never saw it that way. She expected Lyah to take her demeaning words and become Princess Diana within the next breath. And even then, it wouldn't be enough.

Lyah was tired of hearing her mother's mouth for the night. With her resolve set, she got up from the couch and headed for the front door. "You know, maybe you should focus less on me and more on your failures in life, Mom," Lyah said pointedly.

She wasn't more than halfway out the door when her mother snarled, "You're one of them."

Lyah stood frozen for a split second before slamming the door behind her and stepping out into the chilly night.

Enough was enough.

The neighborhood was quiet. There weren't signs that someone had heard their verbal altercation inside. Or rather, cared.

Good, she thought.

Eyes cast down, Lyah headed west. Walking down the dimly lit pathway, Lyah knew the path to his house like the back of her hand. When the going got tough, it's where she sought comfort. It was the only place she felt welcomed nowadays. She hadn't known him long, but he was a refreshing light in her tunnel. At least until she decided to leave, that is.

Lyah shivered and folded her arms as a light breeze passed. She sacrificed getting her jacket from her room before leaving. She'd rather deal with the cold outside than to stay anywhere near her mother's frigid heart.

Since graduating, Lyah wasn't sure where her next stop would be. She had nowhere to go. There was no college in her future. There was no steady love in her life. She had no skills. She barely made it through high school with a 2.8 GPA. It wasn't that she wasn't smart. Her heart just wasn't in it anymore. To prove to anyone that she was better than they thought because the truth was, they were going to believe what they wanted regardless of how much she tried. She'd been down that road. She made a U-turn long ago.

Lyah could see his house in the distance. He still lived with his parents, although he was planning to leave in the fall. Where to, she wasn't sure. She had contemplated asking him whether she could come, but she knew better. Where he was going and where she was likely to end up would be on two separate sides of the spectrum.

Walking up to his front door, she turned the knob and entered. He had always assured her that his door stayed open. His parents were never home. He had no sibling, and to be honest, there wasn't anything worth stealing in the house.

Lyah had a strange feeling tonight, though. Her heart felt heavy with the eeriness coming from the house. It was dark on the bottom level. The only light to guide her way was from the fixture above the paint-peeling stairs. Slowly, she ascended the steps, the creak of each step the only indication of a moving being in the house.

At the top of the stairs, she paused. The bathroom to her left had the lights on, and she could hear the shower running. Any other day, she would've joined him without notice. Tonight, however, she only wanted to sleep. She headed to the closed bedroom door and turned the knob.

Lyah froze. Most of his furniture was missing. His closet door was wide open and inside was empty apart from his bed. Around it sat suitcases seemingly filled and ready to go. She stepped into the room a little further, her eyes scanning the scene before her. She had no idea he was leaving sooner rather than later.

Was he going to leave without telling her? Then again, did she even have a right to know?

She jumped when she felt strong arms circling her waist. She shivered when he whispered in her ear. "You could've joined me in the shower."

She turned around and stared at those deep brown eyes.

James O 'Riley.

He was somebody who kept to himself during high school. He was your typical average boy next door and had the looks to show for it. His brown eyes were mostly kind but sometimes distant. But she always felt secure around his tall frame.

James was a great listener and even better at making her forget her problems, if even for a fleeting moment. It didn't hurt that he was great in bed. She never felt more for him than a deep sense of caring, however.

In another lifetime, she could see herself falling for a guy like him. But her reality was different. With their arrangement, they promised to keep things only on a surface level. They'd never gone deeper. They never ventured into their personal lives, nor did they talk about love. What they had was like a temporary business deal, and she was okay with that. She couldn't do deep. She wasn't sure if she ever could.

James began placing tender kisses along her neck when she asked, "You're leaving?"

He paused slightly before mumbling into her neck, "I wasn't sure how to tell you. I wasn't even sure I was going to leave so soon."

"Where are you going?" she asked as he let go of her to go to his bed and sit. A pile of clothes sat on the corner but not enough to evade space. He dropped his towel and began to dress fully. Briefly turning to her, he gave her a sad look before pulling on a white t-shirt.

Prologue

He wasn't going to tell her, she gathered from that look. She understood, though, and she wasn't going to disrupt his plans. Instead, she made her way up to him and hugged him tightly. His arms circled her, making her feel warm and oddly protected.

She kissed him on the lips hungrily, and he responded with just as much greed. When the back of his legs hit the edge of the bed, he landed with her on top of him, their mouth still fused. Grabbing the back of her hair, he deepened the kiss, his tongue playing tag with hers. After a few minutes, she came up for air and smiled gingerly at him. He smiled back, but it didn't reach his eyes.

"Tonight, I just want to sleep. Can you hold me?"

"Anything for you," he answered. Lyah quirked her eyebrows at him but said nothing. Scooting further onto the bed, she lay on her side, facing him as he came to lay beside her.

Stroking her hair, he stared at her, and she did the same. They did this often: silent communication. He was sad to go, she gathered, but he had likely felt he had no other choice.

"When?" she whispered. James played with her lips for a few moments before answering.

"Tomorrow." It was all they said for the rest of the night. She closed her eyes and welcomed his warm arms until she couldn't feel them anymore. Her dreams always stayed consistent. Empty, dark, and listless. But tonight, she accepted it. She was happy to fall into the pits of darkness to escape her running thoughts.

Tomorrow was a new day. Tomorrow, she'd have to find another outlet. Tomorrow, she'd run. She'd run far, far away.

Chapter One

Lyah

Two years later

God, she loved the dress, but damn was it annoying. If it rode up one more time, she'd consider doing some damage to it. She didn't care whether she was in a bar or not. For the umpteenth time that night, she pulled the sides down as she scoured the tables for something—or rather someone.

Mr. Tall, Dark, and Handsome had been avoiding her all night, she suspected. Lyah wasn't dumb. She felt he wasn't particularly keen on her advances, but she refused to let him escape her sights tonight. She wanted something from him, and she was hell-bent on getting it. Never one to give up, she looked around for his dark curls before smiling to herself.

Ignoring the dirty looks from the female patrons and the suggestive looks from the opposite sex, Lyah hurried to the bar's dark corner where her brooding hero stayed hidden. He didn't see her approach from behind.

Throwing her arms around his neck, Lyah pressed herself against his back and whispered in his ear, “Where did you go so fast?”

He jumped from her touch and yanked her off him a bit roughly. Oh, he was angry. Seething even, if the dark look in his eyes were any indication. He wasn’t in the mood for her antics tonight. Ignoring his flare, she put on her best pout and tried to touch his arm, but he smacked it away. She let out an “ouch,” not expecting the sting that came from it. Abusive much?

“What the hell does it mean to you when someone says to leave them alone? I don’t fuck with prostitutes. Leave me the hell alone!” His words came out a lot harder with each sentence and catching the other customers’ attention at the bar. The bartender gave her a stern look as if telling her he wouldn’t mind throwing her out. It wouldn’t be the first time.

Mr. Tall, Dark, and Handsome pushed his chair back with a loud scrape and left her cradling her hand as he walked out the bar. Lyah wanted to yell at him about his misinterpretation. She hadn’t slept with anyone in over a year and a half, but she wasn’t about to waste her breath. They always thought she was a prostitute, but she never gave them any reason to think otherwise.

“Well, that most certainly didn’t go well,” she mumbled to herself. Giving up, she hopped on the chair he abandoned. It was still warm with his body heat. Most of the customers had already lost interest in her debacle and had gone on to nurse their drinks.

All except one.

He seemed a bit drunk by the way he was two-stepping his way over. Lyah giggled as she noticed he slipped off the chair as he tried to sit beside her. He wasn't exactly her type with a crooked nose and freckles plastering his face. His eyes were a black hole, and his hair looked like he never quite understood what hair care products were. He would have to do for the night.

Ah, Target #32.

"Just wanted you to know I would never turn down anythin' from you," he slurred as he appreciated the way the dress barely passed her mid-thigh. She wanted to roll her eyes, but instead, she gave him a flirty smile. He seemed like an easy target. Why the hell not?

"Nothing?" Lyah flirted. He was already scooting—or trying to—the chair closer to her while still nursing his beer. His breath smelled awful and reeked of alcohol, which indicated he probably was drinking for at least a couple of hours already.

Lyah wrinkled her nose at his smell and proximity but forced herself not to comment on it. She needed to stay focused on the end goal. "Nothin'." She couldn't quite place his accent or whether it was the liquor tuning it for him. Southern, perhaps?

It wasn't until a little after two in the morning she felt the urge to go back to her room at the motel down the street. After nursing two beers herself and trying to coax her unsuspecting drunken participant, Lyah felt like the night was a bust. If she had to hear him talk about himself anymore, she'd consider drowning herself in her drink.

She got up to leave in the middle of him still yammering about some trip to Colorado he needed to take for business—whatever that was— and started toward the door. She turned around and noticed he had begun to follow her, unfortunately. A little annoyed, she stopped as he stammered toward her with a lazy yet unappealing smile.

"Where you goin'?" he slurred.

"Home. And I'd prefer it if you didn't follow," Lyah answered. Hoping he got the point, she turned away only for him to tug her arm.

"Lemme come witchu," he said. "Or at least drive me to your place to crash until I call my men?"

His men? She shook her head. No way in hell was that happening tonight. Or ever.

"Maybe you should call your 'men' now. Or an Uber, perhaps?"

"What's the matter, babe? You don't want me to know where you live? I promise I'll take real good care of ya tonight," he winked at her as he shuffled closer but took a misstep and fell to his face.

A pile of cash dropped from his pants pocket, catching Lyah's interest. From what she could see, there were several hundred-dollar bills. Enough to get the hell out of the city and away from him. Realizing his mistake, he swiped it up quickly and stuffed it back into his pocket. Looking down at his pitifully drunken self, Lyah promptly devised a plan in her head.

With newfound interest, she offered him a hand, which he gladly took.

"You know what? Let's grab a motel room. It's getting late, and

I may need someone strong to protect me," Lyah offered, her voice dripping with honey.

His suggestive smile widened. "I can be all that and more."

Lyah swallowed the sarcasm that threatened to leave her lips. "Just come," she said as she made her way out of the bar.

"I can do that too."

She ignored him and watched from the corner eye as he stumbled and tried to keep up with her with his eyes half shut. He was close to passing out. She needed to get him in a room. Fast.

The motel was a hole-in-the-wall but was a place to stay temporarily until her next move. If everything went according to plan, she'd be out before he realized she wasn't a drunken dream.

Making her way to the dingy motel lobby, she turned to her target of the night and smiled. "A real man pays for the room he's about to get laid in."

At some point during the walk, Lyah decided to get another room for them. She wouldn't dare let him know where her room was or that she even had one at the motel. It only cost fifty bucks a night.

The motel clerk gave her a once-over look but said nothing as Lyah gave her the information she needed. Her target took the bait. Sloppily, he rummaged through his pockets for the cash as if he forgot where he put it. After checking the same pocket twice, he finally pulled out a one-hundred-dollar bill.

The clerk took it and gave them a key without so much as a thank you.

The clerk must've been new because she wasn't there when Lyah checked in days ago. Not dwelling on it, she made her way to the room with her drunken guest for the night.

The room looked exactly like hers but reversed. It was small with a countertop refrigerator and a mounted TV above the desk in front of the bed. The pale pink wall color reminded her of something she watched on television that was depicted in the 1980s. It was gag worthy.

"You don't mind if I—"

Lyah turned to find him passed out in the single loveseat near the window. One shoe laid on the floor, and the other hung from his foot as he spread across the couch on his stomach.

"This will be easier than I thought," she mumbled to herself.

Quietly, she made her way to him to check if he was really asleep. A grunt followed by a loud snore confirmed her suspicions. With tentative fingers, she slid her hand in the pocket he had pulled out the hundred-dollar bill. Feeling a bundle, she slowly pulled it out to find a handful of hundreds.

Jackpot.

Mentally, Lyah danced, but she couldn't celebrate for long. She debated whether she should risk looking for more.

Might as well, she thought as she slipped her hand into his other pocket. She frowned when she pulled out a squishy package with what felt like hard sand. It took her a few moments of staring at the white substance to figure out what it was.

Eyes enlarged, Lyah pulled out two more bags from his pocket, each a little larger than a fun-sized M&Ms bag.

His pockets were deep; she thought as she weighed the three bags of drugs in her hand. She'd never done drugs minus a little weed, nor did she plan on it anytime soon. She'd never sold on the streets either.

What could she do with the bags?

"First time for everything," Lyah mumbled. If she was going to steal it, she might as well profit from it.

Careful not to wake him, she slipped the cash and drugs into her bra, taking out the stuffing she had in there for looks. She knew it would come in handy someday.

Before taking off, Lyah decided to freshen up in the bathroom. No use in walking out shabby.

She closed the door behind her, splashed cold water on her face, and patted her cheeks to stay alert.

Taking advantage of people was exhausting.

It wasn't like she chose this life—okay, maybe she did—but she had no other choice. Being on the streets for two years alone was enough to make anyone want to off themselves. But Lyah wasn't just anyone.

She was built differently.

Not a tear had shed since the last time she let someone penetrate her forces. She promised never to let anyone else take advantage of her. That's why she did it to them first.

Lyah looked at the unkempt mirror and smiled. Tonight, she'd leave the motel and find a better one across town after hitching a ride. The stack in her bra was at least two bands. It would last her about a week or two until her next target.

Finally, she could afford a good meal, maybe get a new wardrobe or two. The dress she had on was great for clubbing and catching targets, but frankly, she was tired of wearing it. Not to mention, it was irritating.

Feeling sticky just thinking about it, she made her way out of the bathroom and abruptly stopped as she stared at the barrel of a pistol in her face.

"You thought chu'd get away with it, huh? I may be out of it, but I'm not stupid," her target said as he rubbed the sleep from his eye.

Could've fooled me, she thought. She didn't dare say it out loud.

"Who do you work for? Is it Presley, the little shit? That's my load, and he ain't gettin' it. Give it back now."

Who the hell was Presley? Such a preppy name for a potential drug dealer.

Lyah knew it was dumb, but if his half-lidded eyes were any indication, she'd guess that the barely standing man with the pistol in his hand was two seconds away from falling to the floor.

She decided to try her luck before her nerves got the best of her. Inching closer, Lyah put on a slightly uneasy smile. "I don't know what you're talking about, but maybe we should have a seat. I didn't finish what I started before you fell asleep on me."

Her answer earned her an unexpected blow to the side of her

head with the pistol. Swearing to herself, she cradled her throbbing head. She needed an escape and fast. He had her with her back to the bathroom on the opposite side of the room. He stood right in front of the path to the room door.

"I don't play about my money and or my powder. I don't think you understand who the fuck you're dealing with. Get on the bed." He sounded soberer now than he did a minute ago. His slurred speech was almost gone, and his words were clearer. Was he playing her?

He motioned with the gun for her to move to the bed and sit, which she had no choice but to oblige. She gulped when he approached her, the gun pushing closer to her face, his eyes looking more alert. He licked his dry lips and appraised her body.

"I also don't play about sex. Now, I believe you owe me something. You want my money? You're gonna have earn it."

If he were smart, he'd take the drugs and money from her now, but alas, he was thinking with the wrong head.

Lyah's eyes carefully accessed the bulge staring at her face. She didn't make a move, nor did she flinch when he began to unbutton his jeans.

This part was familiar to her. She didn't have sex with these men; many have tried and failed to get her to do what she didn't want. Usually, she'd take this time to "get comfortable" in the bathroom and leap out of a window, or she'd "forget" something outside and never return. Most of the time, they were high or drunk on their own accord, and she'd walk right out the door with her "earnings" for the night. But being caught wasn't her game. She always found a way out of it; this time should be no different.

Except it was.

It wasn't until the pistol had found its way under her chin and his hands began to skate across her chest did panic start to set in. She's really done it now. She needed a plan and fast.

"Wait!" Lyah exclaimed, momentarily distracting him. "I'll give it all back. I-I have it in my bra."

If she had never seen a sinister smile before, she definitely did then. "Oh, I plan to get everything that's mine. Take off your clothes before I rip it off."

The pressure of the pistol hardened as she started to tremble a little. There was no escape at this point.

What had she gotten herself into? Her control had slipped, and now she was paying for it. This was supposed to be an easy job.

Still determined not to make him see her slight panic, Lyah slowly lowered the straps of her dress and halved it by her waist, her white bra the only thing still between them.

The baggies and money spilled into her lap as she undressed her shoulders. With her eyes still on him, she noticed his gaze had trailed to the baggies on her lap. His grip on the pistol faltered for only a second.

That second was her chance.

Saying a quick prayer, Lyah swiftly picked up the bags and threw them across the room, two of them bursting as they came in contact with the edge of the television.

He leaped for the bags, the pistol falling from his hand onto the bed beside her, but he was too late. White powder dusted the entire dresser and parts of the floor.

Lyah grabbed the cash and the gun and made a run for the front door, but a loud growl had momentarily paralyzed her.

Without notice, he grabbed the back of her head and slammed it against the closed door, causing her to fall to the floor. The pistol slid into the corner of the room. A burst of pain seeped through her head, and she struggled to lift herself from the ground.

"You thought you could win one over on me, huh? Do you know how much fuckin' money you just cost me?!" he shouted. His dark eyes were aflame. If she didn't get out quick, there'd be nothing but trouble.

He lifted a boot and kicked her in her chest. She collapsed again and coughed up blood into her hand. He hurried to grab the pistol and pointed it at her head as she lay still on the floor.

"I should've killed you when I had the chance," he said as he stood over her.

Thinking quick, Lyah saw her opportunity to kick him in the groin with the heel of her shoe.

"Fuck!" he yelled as he doubled over in pain.

Without thinking, Lyah grabbed the cash and tore through the door, running as fast as she could down the hall and ignoring the pain shooting through her body. She could hear him trying to catch up with her as she barreled out the motel gates and onto the street.

A fresh patch of air hit her chest, and it wasn't until she looked down at herself did she realize she was still half-naked. Pulling her dress up, she searched for a place to hide.

A shot rang out behind her, and she stumbled as she tried to see how far he was. She was in the line of fire though he didn't seem to see her as he looked in another direction.

"You can't run forever, you thieving bitch!"

But she could damn well try.

Lyah dove beside a station wagon that was sandwiched beside another car when another shot zipped past her head and into the window. The bullet shattered the glass and her eardrum. She clutched her ears as they continued to ring for a while.

She covered her head as glass shards bounced off her head. The ringing finally settled in her ears in place of silence for a moment, and she wondered where he had gone. With a quick shuffle to the back of the car, Lyah craned her neck to see if he was close. She gasped when she realized he was on the other side.

"Come out, come out, wherever you are…" he sang as glass crunched beneath his feet. "This'll be a lot easier if you come on out now. You see, I coulda forgave you for stealing the money, but you fucked up my cash flow with the coke, not to mention my reputation. You're gonna pay for that."

Looking across the quiet street, Lyah thought out a plan to dash as he got closer but stopped short when a shout from one of the motel rooms caught both of their attention.

"What happened to my car!"

Lyah could hear footsteps moving away and used that distraction to catch her breath. Should she run now?

"I suggest you find your way back into that motel room, or I blow that head of yours off!"

Lyah snuck a peek at the unsuspecting savior and saw him in front of an open room door, his hands slowly going up in surrender. If she weren't in such a panic, she'd mentality berate his PRINCETON sweater and overly baggy jeans. He looked timid with an oversized pair of glasses perched on his face. The only thing that looked nice was his short golden-brown hair, although even that was pushing it as it sat haphazardly on his head as if he'd just woken up in a panic.

Not her type, but if she didn't make it through this alive, no one else ever would be.

But what was a guy like that doing in such a sketchy area? He certainly did not look like a local and seemed to stand out in his preppy-looking clothes.

"You just blew out my driver's side window! What is wrong with you?" He was bold, that was for sure.

"You watch your goddamn mouth. Don't forget who's holding the gun here."

"Kid has balls," Lyah said to herself in approval.

A shouting match ensued between the two, which bought her time to brainstorm her plan better. She could run across the street and be in plain sight and have more of a chance of getting shot or—she looked at the station wagon in appraisal—she could take her chances with the beaten old car.

Thankfully, she had learned how to hotwire a car when she was dating bad-boy Jason freshman year of high school.

With discretion, she opened the passenger car door and slipped in. The door creaked as she tried to close it, causing her to pause momentarily before closing it all the way. She hurried to the driver's side, looked around the floorboards, found what she needed, and then sparked the wires.

The sound of the car huffing on made her heart leap with joy, but it was short-lived.

"Hey! Get out of my car!" Preppy Guy yelled.

It happened so fast, Lyah could only watch in shock from the driver's side as the gun swung in her direction, but he didn't get a chance to fire. Out of nowhere, a brick hit him on the back of the head, and he tumbled to the ground.

Preppy Guy rushed to the driver's side, where she was. "Get the hell out of my car!"

Still paralyzed, she could only stare at him, which only seemed to anger him more. He opened the door and tried to drag her out, but she gripped the steering wheel tight. "I need this, please! He'll kill me!"

"I just hit him on the back of the head with a brick. I'm pretty sure he'll be out looking for the both of us. Now get out of my car!"

A loud groan caught both their attention as the guy rose from the ground with one hand still holding the gun and the other nursing his head. He looked up and saw the two and started toward them, the gun raised.

"Fuck it, scoot over!"

Coming to her senses, Lyah finally let go of the steering wheel and crawled to the passenger side in time for Preppy Guy to jump into the driver's side and punch the gas. Lyah fell back into her seat as a *clink* sounded against his bumper as they drove out of sight.

Chapter Two

Keith

Earlier that day

If his phone rang one more time, he was going to scream. Why he hadn't shut it off was a mystery to him. Perhaps he was hoping that one call he knew wasn't coming would somehow defy his expectations.

She wasn't going to call.

Keith pushed the weight of his emotions out of his mind for the last time as he drove toward the outskirts of rural Pennsylvania.

Driving out of state was one thing. Driving across the country to Las Vegas to confess his undying love to a woman he wasn't sure loved him back was another. Not to mention, he was planning on intercepting her wedding if needed.

Talk about a turn for dramatics.

It was unusual for Keith to act in such a rash way. The small-town college kid held a life of slow pacing, one where no one knew he existed if they didn't need him for something. He had a normal family, a normal upbringing, a normal—well, everything.

Boring is what he called it.

Except in the last couple of months since Tally had broken it off with him, he started to take a turn for the worse. Feeling as though his life was passing by and he was stagnant, he took a semester to focus on himself, much to his parents' dismay.

When he heard about Tally's decision to get married to a guy she'd only known for a few months after their breakup, it was like Keith's life imploded. Suddenly, it was like his eyes had opened to the world, and he felt suffocated in his state.

He decided to fight for Tally and to show the world that he was not stagnant and boring.

Without much thought or notice to anyone, Keith dived into his car and set out for Las Vegas to tell her what a huge mistake she was making. He tried calling her on several occasions, leaving messages about his feelings toward her and his thoughts on her decision to get married. For once, he didn't feel afraid to show her how everything had affected him.

Tally was supposed to be it for him. He was supposed to marry her someday. She had fit in his life like a perfect glove, and her leaving had crippled the path he thought his life was destined to follow.

The phone's shrill cut his thoughts, and Keith looked over at it in annoyance before finally pressing the answer button. Driving an old 1979 station wagon his dad passed to him, he wasn't privy to Bluetooth that most cars had nowadays, but he did have Air Pods he struggled to get out of his pockets while maneuvering the wheel.

"*Hellllooo?*"

It was his seventeen-year-old brother, Mick.

With a sigh, Keith answered, "I'm here. Sorry, I was fishing for my Air Pods."

"*Yeah, like that's the issue. Where the hell are you? Mom and Dad have been freaking out over here because you won't answer anyone's call. What's going on?*"

"I'm on the road. Don't expect me for a few days. Maybe a week or two."

"*Way to be forthcoming and not cryptic. What do you mean you're on the road? Aren't you supposed to be in class or something?*"

Apparently, his parents were so ashamed of his much-needed break, they hadn't informed anyone else despite the two-month gap he had told them.

"Just tell Mom and Dad that I am fine, and I'll be back in a week or two. I'm heading over to Las Vegas."

"*Vegas?!*" Mick exclaimed in his ear, causing Keith to cringe.

Not ready to delve into the backstory, Keith rushed him off the phone. "I'll explain when I get back. If you call again and I don't pick up, I am fine. Until then, try to keep Mom and Dad calm. Bye."

"*This isn't about Tally, is it? Because—*"

Keith ended the call with a sigh of relief. Having gotten that off his chest, he mustered the courage to finally turn off his phone and focus on the GPS he had installed on the dashboard.

With a few hundred dollars in his pocket and a credit card limit he'd likely never use that his parents controlled, he had all the means to stay away for at least a week. To save money on hotels, he planned only to stay at the cheapest motels he could find along the way. Considering it was a long journey across the country, there would likely be many. And if things really weren't looking bright, he had packed a blanket and pillow to sleep in the backseat of the car.

The world was at his fingertips. He thought about all the things he wanted to say to Tally when they finally met. Would she be surprised or grateful that he came to confess his love for her? Would she see it as romantic as she did in the movies that they used to watch together? Would she welcome him with open arms?

Or was this all in vain?

Keith shook the negative thoughts from his mind. She would love the gesture, he knew it. She barely knew the guy she was marrying, and when she finally came to her senses, he would be the one waiting with open arms.

Thoughts of how everything would go down continued to swirl in his mind as he drove for several more hours before his eyes became hooded.

By the time he had decided to stop at a motel, he had reached a small town just outside Pennsylvania. He pulled into a mostly deserted lot of the Wallow Motel and parked. Looking around the dark area, it seemed relatively uninhabited, except for a few cars.

Though wary of the quiet area, Keith got out and headed to the front office. Looking around the small room after he finished with the clerk as he waited for his key card, he noted how much it reminded him of those vacant motels he often saw in horror movies.

A shiver ran down his spine as the lady returned with his key.

"Here's your key," she said deadpanned. Without so much as an "Enjoy your stay!" she went back to her computer, completely ignoring Keith's presence.

If this were a horror movie, she'd be one of those creepy unfriendly hotel owners that watch people get cut up in their room.

Shaking his head, Keith made his way to his room. Luckily, the window faced his car in the parking lot, so he'd be able to see if anyone tried to steal it.

He laughed at the thought. Anyone stealing a 1979 station wagon in this era was either crazy or desperate. He could probably walk faster than the car could drive.

Keith covered his mouth as an unsuspecting yawn escaped his lips.

"I'll just lay down for a second," Keith said as he flopped on the bed on his back. Usually, he would've dusted the sheets and gone for an extra pair of clothes out of his car, but the sleep was drawing in so heavy, he could barely lift his head from the mattress.

In what seemed like seconds, he was out like a light.

A loud *pop* jolted Keith from the bed. He tripped over his feet, and fell to the floor. It sounded like a firework had just gone off outside his window.

"Who's lighting fireworks at this time of night?"

Another *pop* sounded, and it took a moment for him to realize it wasn't fireworks. It sounded like gunfire, though drastically different from his grandfather's hunting shotgun that he often used when Keith was younger.

With his heart nearly pounding through his chest, Keith looked around his room to see if there were any bullet holes in the wall. There were none. The shots sounded close enough to burst through his door, however.

He crept his way to the window and gasped when he saw his car window was shattered from afar. Without thinking, he swung open the door and shouted, "What happened to my car!"

Keith stopped in his tracks when a gun raised to his face. Immediately, he threw his hands up in surrender, but his eyes surveyed his car in horror. His father was going to kill him. Never mind the gun pointed to his face, if his father ever saw what happened to his precious family inheritance, he would strange him. No—downright torture.

Keith could take his chances with a gun to his face if it meant never facing his father again.

"I suggest you find your way back into that motel room, or I blow that head of yours off!"

Taking a good look at the scruffy and angry stranger, he had no doubt he would do such a thing. But the fear of bringing back the car to his dad with a shattered window frightened him more than the gun pointed to his head.

Keith found himself saying, “You just blew out my driver’s side window! What is wrong with you?”

Stepping closer, the man seemed to get even angrier. “You watch your goddamn mouth. Don’t forget who’s holding the gun here.”

Close up, he could see the bloodshot eyes and the slight limp he had. Was he drunk?

Either way, Keith couldn’t stop his mouth from running. “You’re deranged! Who shoots out a window to someone’s car for fun? Do you know how much that costs to repair? My dad is going to kill me!”

“I can give two shits about your daddy’s car. I got business to take care of. I suggest you heed my warning.”

Looking into the barrel of the gun, Keith realized he was talking himself into a deeper grave. What was he thinking talking back to an obviously drunk and gun-friendly stranger in the middle of the night? And where were the cops? Surely, someone would’ve reported the shots by now.

“Look, we can talk about this. Just put down the gun—”

The familiar exaggerated huff of his car starting caught his attention. In the front seat was a woman he had no idea was there. Was she the person this man had shot after?

Nonetheless, it looked as if she were about to steal his car.

Not on his watch.

“Hey! Get out of my car!” Keith yelled.

The gun swung in her direction, and without thinking, Keith took the opportunity presented to him. Picking up a broken brick from the flowerbed near his door, he reached up and struck the man over the head, successfully landing an impact.

The man fell to the ground with a groan, the gun still clutched in his hand. Rushing to his car before she decided to take off, Keith yelled, “Get the hell out of my car!”

She looked scared and paralyzed, he realized. It was a split second, but he took in her slightly ripped, barely-there, colorful sequin dress and her haphazard look. She had a bruise resting on the top of her forehead, and her makeup was running down her face. She looked worse for wear.

Was she a hooker?

Snapping back to reality, she finally acknowledged his persistence, saying, “I need this, please! He’ll kill me!”

So, that man was after her.

Keith couldn’t believe his ears. She was refusing to get out of *his* car? Like he didn’t just incapacitate the guy with a brick.

Granted, she did have a good reason.

“I just hit him on the back on the head with a brick. I’m pretty sure he’ll be out looking for the both of us. Now get out of my car!”

They both blanched when a loud groan sounded from the man as he began to stir. He got up and looked at the two, raising his gun.

Keith really didn’t have time for this. As a last-ditch effort, he yelled, “Fuck it, scoot over!”

She practically threw herself into the passenger seat, no questions asked, as Keith hopped in and stepped on the gas, speeding out of the motel parking lot. A loud *clink* sounded from the rear of his car, causing them both to jump.

Was it a bullet?

Looking through the rearview mirror, he saw the man standing there in the middle of the street, slowly shrinking away as they descended further down the deserted stretch of pavement.

After getting herself situated adequately in her seat, she leaned back with a sigh of relief. "Phew! Thought we were goners for a minute there." She had the nerve to gleam at him. "You saved my life."

Keith looked at her incredulously. "Saved you? You almost stole my car and left me for dead!"

To his annoyance, she waved him off. "That's water under the bridge now. No need to bring up the past."

If Keith wasn't speeding down the road like Speedy Gonzalez, he might've stared at her like she had two heads. "Who the hell are you?"

"You swear a lot for a timid looking guy."

Keith furrowed his eyebrows though he knew she was right. If his mother heard his mouth, she'd have his tongue.

But timid? He was quiet at times, but timid would imply scared and wimpy. He felt offended.

"Who are you?" Keith repeated. "What did he want?"

He clocked her clothes again, his silent inquiry from earlier nagging him.

"It's not important."

"Damn right, it's important! We could've gotten killed!"

"But we didn't! We're good now, thanks to you," she said with a grateful smile tugging at her lips as if the situation was no big deal.

His face started to heat. At any moment, he'd explode like a volcano. "What did he want?" Keith hesitated before saying the next part. "Was that your pimp?"

It was her turn to be offended. "Pimp? I'm not a prostitute, jackass!"

"Could've fooled me! You owe him money? Is that it?" he bit back.

Lyah clammed up and folded her arms. "It's none of your business."

Keith couldn't help but scuff. He couldn't believe this woman! Here he was driving them away from danger, and this is how she repaid him? "Yeah, right. It's none of my business. You getting my window shot and attempting to steal my car isn't my business. Him turning the gun on me and forcing me to flee my motel room isn't my business! I've known you for mere minutes, and already my life is upside down. Damn right, it's my business!"

Keith heaved with anger, but she sat silent for a moment, defiance written on her face. "Let me out of the car, I'll find my own fucking way."

"Gladly!"

The car came to a screeching halt on the side of the dark road. It looked like they were in the middle of nowhere: no buildings or signs of life anywhere besides the occasional twinkle of the airplane lights in the sky.

But that wasn't his problem. The sooner she got out of his hair, the sooner he can put all of this mess behind him and be on his way.

Stepping out of the car with a scowl, she bent to his level. "Your car is crap anyway."

She slammed the creaky door shut with so much force, it rocked a bit.

"Good fucking riddance!" Keith pressed the gas and took off, leaving her shrinking in his rearview mirror, much like he did their attacker earlier.

Finally, he felt like he was free. It was like a weight had lifted off his shoulder. How dare she interrupt his trip?

The nerve of her!

In a matter of minutes, she had thrown his life into a curveball. He had so many questions, but he knew he would never find an answer anytime soon. Instead, he focused on the road ahead for another motel in sight. Thankfully, he hadn't taken anything significant out of his car when he checked in. Having been too tired to carry his duffel bag, he decided to catch a quick nap and hightail it out of the city.

There went that plan.

He drove for what seemed like hours but was more like a couple minutes and spied a desolate gas station to his left. Looking at his tank, he figured he'd stop by and fill up and try to find something to cover his now permanently opened window.

Keith pulled up to a pump and parked but then realized he couldn't turn it off. His keys weren't in the ignition.

Irritation began to build again. He forgot she hotwired the car.

Who does that anymore?

Keith looked around at the floorboards and spied two cables wrapped around each other. Sticking his key into the ignition with it hotwired didn't seem like a good idea though it may have done nothing but make his job more manageable. In hindsight, he knew nothing of cars besides what little he did for the wagon, so his judgment wasn't the best.

Carefully, he unwrapped the wires, and immediately, the car shut off. A beat of sweat he didn't know had formed dropped from his temple.

Taking a solid minute to catch his breath, he surveyed the battered gas station. Dirty white paint was chipping off the wooden structure outside, and the pavement was barely there. It looked like it was ready to cave in on itself.

Nevertheless, Keith used the open sign outside the entrance as a welcome. The buzzing light flickered outside as he made his way to the door.

"You got any change?" A homeless-looking man emerged from the gas station's shadowed corner, causing Keith to jump in fright.

The old man looked ready to fall at any moment with his slightly hunched figure. He was excessively hairy around his face, with a sprinkle of gray lining his beard and the edges of his hairline.

Fishing for a dollar bill, he handed it to the man. If he wasn't on the road trip, Keith would've offered more, but he wasn't sure the costs he was set to endure, especially after what happened earlier.

The man looked at it in disgust and scuffed. Without another word, he descended back into the shadows like a reaper.

"Uh…" For a moment, Keith stood there, wondering what the hell just happened before shaking his head and making his way inside.

Since he couldn't afford a window repair at a time like this, he decided to look for some durable plastic to stick on the driver's side window if it rained unexpectedly. Driving with a wet interior was something he did not look forward to. He'd have to find a way to get it fixed before returning home, even if it cost what money he had saved.

The store was small and didn't carry much, but Keith wasn't expecting more. He was able to find some off-brand garbage bags and tape for his car. He picked up a few snacks and drinks as well for the road. Carrying his load to the register where an uninterested old man stood staring off into space, Keith decided to make a bathroom run while he had the chance.

Squeezing himself into the one stall box bathroom, he did his business but stood in front of the mirror to observe his appearance after.

He wasn't one to place all his effort into his looks. He was always comfortable with his new golden-brown locks and his black-rimmed glasses perched on the bridge of his nose. He hated tight clothes, which meant his go-to always consisted of a pair of loose jeans and a sweater. He usually loved his look.

But staring into the mirror, he wondered if he really did look timid. Was that why his circle ran small? Did Tally think his looks weren't up to par? Did he seem too wimpy?

Keith had seen her new boyfriend—*fiancé*—from Instagram photos. He was everything Keith was not. He was the definition of tall, dark, and handsome. He could've been a model if he wanted.

Keith scrunched his face in disgust, remembering stalking his page. He probably had no personality. Most pretty people didn't.

Pushing Tally—and *him*—out of his mind, he made his way back to the register where the old guy still stood, but this time, reading through a newspaper.

The old guy rang up Keith's items and the gas, and not long after, Keith was back in his car. He dumped his contents in the car and stood outside as he filled his tank. Looking around to pass the time, something caught his eye on the opposite side of the road.

Squinting in the dark, a gleam from the reflection of the streetlight bounced off her dress as she paced forward.

There was no way. It was her.

It looked like she was limping, but a closer look showed that one of her heels was missing.

How had that happened in the short time he left her on the side of the road?

She hugged herself as she kept her head low. From far away, she resembled a child, cold and frail, maybe even a bit afraid?

Keith turned away, a thickness in his throat forming. The truth was, he felt terrible given how she looked. He had left an unsuspecting girl on the side of the road with a madman out there. She could've been kidnapped, raped, or killed in the dark, and nobody would have known or cared. He'd be at fault for not helping her when he had the chance.

His mother taught him better than that.

But this girl was also a stranger. Maybe she was bad news, too? Considering the mess she was in, his judgment wouldn't be far off.

Keith wasn't sure what it was, but his gut was telling him otherwise.

Was he feeling sorry for her even after she almost got him killed? No, he couldn't put the blame all on her. Had he stayed inside and kept his mouth shut, he wouldn't be running with her. But then, he wouldn't have saved her, either.

All the anger he felt earlier had seemed to dissolve in a matter of a second.

Miraculously, it was like his foot had propellers, and he couldn't stop walking in her direction. Even with the man from the shadows emerging as she grabbed the handle of the gas station door, he pushed through his unease.

"You got change?" Keith heard the old man ask as he drew closer.

She looked up and was about to answer when Keith interrupted. "She has nothing. She's with me."

Frightened, she jumped in shock and looked behind her with

wide eyes. Before she could react further, Keith grabbed her arm and took her to his car, which she thankfully did not resist.

Yet.

Chapter Three

Lyah

Lyah was shocked to find him behind her. She hadn't been paying much attention as she wandered on the street, the wind whipping her exposed skin and causing a shiver every now and then.

To say she was lost and feeling a bit crappy would be an understatement. After he drove off, she flicked him off, her "I can do anything myself" attitude strong and confident. But it took less than ten minutes of walking in the quiet darkness to realize she was actually scared.

Her travels sometimes called for hitching a ride or taking public transport but out in the open and exposed to her failed target, and other unsuspecting people in the desolate area didn't sit right in her stomach.

At some point, the owl hoots and the shuffling of leaves on the bare ground got to her, and she began to rush. But as her luck would have it, one of her heels broke. Considering she couldn't walk with it, she decided to toss the one foot and limp the rest of the way until she found a place to crash. Her luck had likely hightailed it long ago.

She happened upon the gas station from afar not long after and decided to use what she could for a bite to eat. If she would be out on the road all night long, she'd need food and water.

Lyah hadn't expected to find *him* there.

All at once, anger warmed her blood, and she halted as he attempted to pull her to the car. Scared or not, Preppy Guy still left her on the street to rot without a second thought.

Halfway to the car, Lyah yanked her arm from his grip with a scowl. "Get your hands off me! I don't need your help!"

Though her demeanor was tired and vulnerable, she refused to let him see that side of her.

"I'm trying to help you!"

Lyah snared, "Yeah, like leaving me on the side of the road was helpful. I don't need you."

He huffed in frustration. "Look, you're the one who wanted to get out the car. And quite frankly, you're irritating and mean and evasive—"

"Then, I don't see what you need from me," Lyah bitterly laughed.

Lyah turned to leave, but he grabbed her again. His grip was firmer than she thought it'd be, but not enough to hurt her.

"What's your name?"

The question caught her off guard. "Why should I tell you?"

"I'm not going to do anything with it."

"What if I don't trust you?"

"Kind of too late for that. I mean, you did almost steal my car and get me killed. You contributed to putting a target on my back. The least you could do is give me your name."

Preppy Guy had a point. That didn't stop her from rolling her eyes, however.

"Are you always going to use that against me?"

He gave her a pointed look, and her standoffish behavior seemed to dissipate. At least he could take what she dished.

His eyes were beautiful. The dull light over the car pump hit his eyes just right, casting a hazel hue.

"Lyah," she found herself saying. "My name is Lyah. Do I get a name, too?"

"I'm Keith." A better name than Preppy Guy, she supposed.

Keith extended a hand that Lyah eyed with suspicion. "Why are you suddenly so nice to me? I thought you couldn't wait to get rid of the 'prostitute.'"

Keith grimaced. "Change of heart, I guess."

"Is that supposed to make us friends?"

Keith frowned but turned away. "Hardly." Opening the passenger side door, gestured for her to get in.

Lyah eyed the passenger seat she sat in less than an hour ago. She realized she had no idea where she—or he for that matter—was going.

“Where are you heading, anyway?”

“Vegas.”

Lyah pursed her lips. Las Vegas was far. What business would he have there?

As if reading her mind, Keith vaguely explained, “I’ve got some business to take care of in Vegas that’s… urgent. Where are you headed?”

Lyah looked around. There was a possibility gun-toting Sam would come back for revenge. It was probably best she get as far away as possible.

“Anywhere but here. Take me to Vegas with you.”

Keith vehemently shook his head. “I’ll drop you off someplace safe, but you are not coming to Las Vegas with me.”

“Maybe I can help with this cryptic business of yours. You get me out of here, and I’ll be at your beck and call.”

Keith stared at her like she had just told him his foot would no longer work. “No.”

Lyah shrugged. “Then, I guess me dying would just have to weigh on your conscience.”

She knew that’s what he had meant when he said he had a sudden change of heart. Maybe she could use that to her advantage.

A moment passed, and with a defeated sigh, Keith said, “Fine. Just get in the car. *Please*.”

Lyah smiled to herself as she finally accepted the open-door invitation. “Don’t mind if I do.”

They didn't speak again as Keith replaced the pump and covered his window with the clear bag he bought from the station. It wasn't until he sat down in front of the wheel that she realized she still needed to get food and drinks.

Before he could start the car, she exclaimed, "Wait! I need to get food."

Keith held up a bag from the back seat. "I bought a few snacks and some water. You'll be fine."

Lyah looked at the bag in consideration but shook her head. "Yeah, no, thank you. I'll get my own stuff."

She got out of the car but realized she was without proper shoes. "You wouldn't happen to have an extra pair of shoes, would you?"

"Driving you is one thing. Wearing my clothes is another. No."

"I didn't ask for clothes. I said *shoes*." Keith sat silent. Lyah groaned in frustration. He was a stubborn one. "Come on, I know you packed extra shoes or even flip flops if you're going to Las Vegas."

"I did, but for me."

"Keith…" Lyah went as far as to push a pout.

Noticeably defeated once again, Keith pointed to the back seat. "I have a pair of flip flops in the back. Do not lose or break them. It's my only pair."

Delighted, Lyah reached into the back seat with no regard to his personal space as her butt had to toot in the air. She could've just grabbed it by opening the back door, but it wouldn't have been much fun.

Annoying him was becoming amusing.

"Found it!" she said in a sing-song voice.

Lyah righted herself and took off her only heel and flung it to the backseat, earning a "Hey!" from Keith. The flip flops were old and tattered with black threading sticking from the sides, but it was just what she needed. Comfort outweighed the style.

She slipped them on but hadn't anticipated how big they would be on her size eight feet.

With a frown, she began, "What size do you wear? These are huge!"

"Take the shoes or leave it," Keith said with finality.

Lyah scrunched her nose at him. "You know, for someone who's looking to clean their conscience, you sure are an ass."

With that, she left the car and headed inside, this time, with her head held high.

The guy never returned from the corner shadows, so she was able to walk right in and get what she wanted. Some Cheetos, a few Hersey bars, some Rice Krispy treats, and a liquor bottle later, Lyah was at the register. The old attendant didn't even bother asking for ID.

When she skipped back to the car, Keith had a peculiar look on his face.

"What?" she asked as she settled the bags between her feet.

"Where did you get money to buy all this?"

Oops. Busted. Lyah forgot he had no idea she had stolen money from her failed target.

"Uhhh… I borrowed it?" Lyah said with an awkward smile. Not even a child would've believed her.

Keith narrowed his eyes. "You stole from him! That's why he was after you!"

"It was only a little bit! I needed it!"

A little bit was a complete understatement.

"And here I was feeling sorry for you!"

Lyah rolled her eyes like it was no big deal. "Can we just go before he somehow pops up?"

Keith gazed at her in disbelief before shaking his head and mumbling something under his breath as he slid the wagon back onto the road.

***

They drove in silence for what seemed like forever. The next motel apparently wasn't for some time according to the GPS, and because of extreme weather conditions as they drove into Ohio, they had to detour off the highway.

"Do you have a jacket?" Lyah asked as she popped a Cheeto into her mouth, her feet propped on the dashboard.

Keith glanced at her, his eyes briefly flickering to her bare feet in disgust then back to the road. "No clothes. I'm not giving you my clothes."

"Why not?" She'd never seen someone so possessive of clothes, let alone a jacket. She knew he had one. She had seen it when she got the flip flops resting under some scattered clothes in the backseat.

"Because I said so. Why can't you just leave it alone?"

"Because I'm cold," Lyah replied matter of fact. There was still a draft coming from the taped window on his side. Though it wasn't freezing outside, the fall nights were getting much cooler.

"No, shit. Besides, don't you have stolen money? You can use it to buy an outfit when we stop."

"Which is when exactly?"

Keith shrugged.

"I don't understand why you're snippy with me when you're the one who invited me back to the car. You didn't see me with anything in my hand or a bag. How do you expect me to have extra clothes lying around? Everything got left at the motel. And since you're not stopping, I can't buy anything."

Lyah could tell Keith was processing what she said because his shoulders sagged. She was definitely winning this game. "Fine. Whatever."

Lyah mentally jumped for joy, though her facial features showed indifference.

"I have a jacket in the back under some clothes. Just the jacket, nothing else until we find somewhere to get more clothes."

Lyah reached into the back and grabbed the black fleece jacket she'd seen earlier and wrapped it around her shoulders. It was big enough to engulf her. Soft to the touch.

It was perfect.

Discretely, she took a whiff of it; the scent of Axe hit her nostrils.

Good taste, she thought.

"Don't ruin it, either. That's my only pair."

"Yeah, because I have plans to toss it down a rabbit hole. You'll be fine. It's not like you're not already wearing a sweater," Lyah said, her voice dripping with sarcasm.

Keith muttered to himself, "I should've just left you at the gas station."

"What was that?" Lyah couldn't help but tease, knowing all too well what he said.

"Nothing!"

She thought so. Moving forward, she attempted to turn on the radio station, but Keith slapped her hand away. "Ow!"

"Don't. Touch. My. Radio."

"You've got issues," Lyah said, cradling her hand. "Why can't I touch anything? It's too quiet in here, and frankly, I don't want to talk to you the entire time I'm in here, and I'm sure you don't either."

"Why do you think? Maybe I want to listen to silence if you'd just shut up!"

"You shut up!"

"No, you—know what? Forget it. Turn on the damn radio. Just leave me alone." Keith gripped the steering wheel so tight; his knuckles were changing colors.

Anger was unbefitting of him. All his yelling was for nothing because it was going through one ear and out the other. She happily turned on the radio, switching the station to a more upbeat pop song. She figured it would most likely irritate him as he looked like someone who enjoyed softer tunes.

"Really?" He said on cue.

Lyah bopped her head to the beat, turning to him. "What? It's good music."

Keith scoffed. "Good? This is utter trash. Nothing beats the fine music of classical 80s and 90s era."

Lyah stopped dancing and looked at him in disgust. "What are you? Forty? Get with the program, old man."

"It's better than this crap. It's like the same lyrics and beats regurgitated over and over again. There's nothing original about these new-age songs besides the samples."

"You might be as old as your ride. How will you ever get through Vegas?"

"I may not fit in, but at least I don't look like a hooker. I could probably let you off at the Red-Light District, and they'd welcome you with open arms."

Low blow. Lyah didn't want to admit that stung, though it wasn't the first time he referred to her as a sex worker. Her clothes were meant to draw particular attention, but she'd never had sex with a stranger since running away from home, nor did she ever sell any part of her body. Her clothes were for one purpose and one purpose only: to catch a target.

Nevertheless, she didn't bother to argue. Instead, she leaned back and peered out the window as an Ed Sheeran song began to play from his speakers.

Chapter Four

Keith

Lyah was awfully quiet for the remainder of the ride. It shouldn't have bothered him like it did, but he couldn't help to think he had gone too far. Sure, she was a thief, possibly homeless, and the way she was dressed was not that far off from what he had seen sex workers wear, but that didn't give him a right to assume—again.

Keith opened his mouth several times to apologize but chickened out last minute. She had reclined the seat and laid with her back to him, her legs tucked in a slight fetal position. She was so small his jacket blanketed over her entire body. Her dark curls covered her face, so he couldn't see if she had fallen asleep or not.

He made a note to apologize when they settled into a motel room.

After another hour of driving, he was able to find a cheap but decent motel in the area. They advertised a seventy-dollar rate on the sign as he pulled into the full parking lot. He hoped they had a spare room or two on short notice.

Shutting off the car, Keith turned to Lyah to see if she had stirred.

She hadn't.

Keith battled himself whether he should leave her in the car while he checked to see if there were any rooms. A soft snore grabbed his attention.

She was fast asleep.

Keith decided to leave her in the car. It wasn't hot, but it wasn't freezing either to warrant any worry about her being uncomfortable with the windows—and plastic—up.

As a precaution, he pulled the key from the ignition just in case she got any funny ideas and slid quietly out of the car.

Making his way to the check-in desk, Keith noted the line of people in front of him.

"Shit," he muttered as he took his place in line. It wasn't exceptionally long given the early morning time, but the motel wasn't entirely big either. With the low rate, they were likely to be gone in no time.

Keith waited for what seemed like hours before stepping in front of a clerk. A middle-aged lady with aging blond hair greeted him with a friendly smile, unlike the last clerk he stood before.

"How can I help you, sir?"

"I'd like 2 rooms, please," Keith said as he pulled out his wallet.

"I'm sorry, sir, but we only have one room left at this time. It has twin beds. Would you care to book that?"

Keith thought for a moment about sharing a room with Lyah and her talking his head off, though he knew he had no choice but to get it. Now was not the time to be picky.

"I'll take it. One night, please."

Keith paid and took the room key from the lady as he made his way back to the car. He opened his door to find Lyah up and scrolling through his cell phone.

"What are you doing with my phone?" he gritted as he grabbed it from her hands and powered it off.

She didn't seem mad anymore because she proceeded to badger him with questions. "Why do you keep your phone off? And who's Tally?" she asked without shame.

"None of your damn business. Keep your hands off my stuff. I got us a room, so can we please get inside?"

Lyah obliged but still felt the need to pester him, it seemed. "Just one room?"

Keith turned to her, a scowl on his face as he took out a duffle bag from the trunk and locked the doors. As they made their way to the rooms lined up outside, Keith said, "Trust me, if I was able to get two, then I would've. Obviously, I couldn't. Now, you're more than welcomed to not sleep in it and let me have the room to myself."

Lyah scuffed. "As if! What's the room number?"

"2A."

She grabbed the keycard from his hand and opened the door to room 2A. It wasn't much different from the last motel room he was in, sighting two beds, a mini-fridge, and a small television in front of the twin mattresses.

The floor looked cleaner as did the sheets, which calmed his nerves a bit. Walking in, he threw his duffle bag on the bed closest to the door and sat down, proceeding to remove his sneakers.

"At least this room is better than the last," Lyah mimicked his thoughts.

He ignored her as he pulled out a few articles of clothing to wear after his shower, which he had already called dibs on in his mind. He stopped for a moment to regard what she would wear to bed. Granted, she was bound to ask until they could find a decent store, but until then, she had nothing else, nor could she continue to wear what she had on.

Without a second thought, Keith pulled out a large black t-shirt from the bottom of the bag and a pair of boxers, and gray sweatpants for her. Though at the time he was packing, he was less than enthusiastic about bringing so many clothes. Now, he was grateful for it.

Lyah, who was sprawled on the bed next to his, got up when he served her folded clothes. She took them tentatively. "What are these for?"

"For bed. I'm taking a shower. You can go after me."

He left her on the bed, still staring at the clothes, probably shocked that he had even offered. Hell, he was surprised himself.

Taking a quick shower and brushing his hair and teeth, he quickly got dressed in his pajamas and exited the bathroom. He stopped abruptly when he noticed Lyah pulling her dress and bra off in a swift motion. She stood with her back to him in nothing but a black thong.

"W-What are you doing?" he blurted.

Lyah craned her neck over her shoulder. "Getting ready for my shower."

Rooted in his spot, he asked, "Why not do that in the bathroom?"

A sly smile etched on her face. "Are you nervous, Keith?"

His name slipped off her tongue for the first time, and he was ashamed to admit he liked the way she said it. It was velvety. "I just think that you should do that in the bathroom. For privacy."

Lyah shook her head and brushed him, carrying the clothes he gave her to her chest, obscuring her exposed skin. She took his towel from his hands as it hung limply from his fingers. "I'll remember that next time."

She shut the door after her, and only then could Keith feel himself breathe. He shook his head to rid of the image of the smooth curve of her back and her plump bottom. By the time she was finished with her shower, Keith was already in bed curled up with his night lamp off, though his eyes were wide open.

He listened as Lyah hummed to herself and shuffled from space-to-space, opening the mini-fridge and turning on the TV as she settled into bed. It cast a blue hue in the room as the news droned about some crimes around the city.

Though he had yet to see her as his back was turned to her bed, Keith knew she wouldn't be asleep for a while. He thought about his earlier promise to apologize, figuring now was the best time.

"Lyah?" he said softly without turning.

"Hmm?" she answered.

"I'm sorry about earlier. About calling you a hooker. I crossed a line—again, and that wasn't right."

Out of all the responses, he thought he would receive; her giggling was not one of them. Turning around, Keith frowned. "What's so funny?"

Lyah pinned him with a smirk. "You? Apologizing? It's cute."

"I don't understand."

"Well, first, thank you for the apology. I accept. Second, hearing you apologize is cute. You seem like such a stubborn hard ass; I just wasn't expecting it. Well, I wasn't expecting you to come back for me, either. Technically, you didn't but—"

"Okay! I get it. I got it off my conscience. Can we go back to not talking?" Keith shuffled back to his previous position with his back to her in embarrassment.

The silence picked up again, minus the soft sounds from the TV. Still, Keith couldn't seem to drift off, no matter how tight he shut his eyes. It was almost like he was aware of everything Lyah was doing. Picking her nails. Shifting in the bed. Turning off her lamp.

It was driving him insane.

"Keith?" Lyah whispered.

He decided to ignore her. Maybe she would think he was asleep.

"Keith?" she said a little louder. "Who's Tally? Keith?"

Frustrated, he twisted his body to her. "I'm trying to sleep."

Through the glow of the TV, he could see her face light up with a smile. “No, you weren’t.”

“How would you know?”

Lyah pointed to his eyes. “There’s no sleep in your eyes. Besides, there was no heavy ‘sleep breathing’ from you. You look like a snorer.”

She was a lot more observant than he thought.

“What the hell is ‘sleep breathing?’”

“You know, that deep, even breathing we do when we’re sleeping? That’s what it is.”

“Huh,” Keith found himself saying as he leaned back, looking at the ceiling.

“So, who’s Tally? Is that why you’re going to Vegas?” Lyah leaned on her elbow to face him. He found himself assessing her in his black t-shirt. Though he couldn’t see the rest of the clothes because she was covered with a blanket, he knew his clothes would be big on her. The shirt probably fit her like a dress.

“It’s none of your business, Lyah.”

“It is if I’m going to Vegas with you.”

“You’re not going to Vegas with me.”

“Yes, I am.”

“I’m dropping you off somewhere else along the way. Don’t you have family in one of these states or something? A friend in the area?”

“I don’t have a family, and I don’t have friends.”

That shut him up. The way she said it held a hint of melancholy though she tried to hide it behind the smile she was currently sporting.

He wanted to pry but considering her deep interest in Tally, he figured it was best they left things where they were. They were strangers still.

His eyes finally started to get tired, and he felt them shut slowly. “You should get some sleep. We leave in a few hours,” he found himself saying.

“Does that mean I’m going to Vegas with you?”

For some reason, the excitement in her voice almost made him feel like a hero. Like he was giving her a purpose. Maybe taking her to Las Vegas wouldn’t be a bad thing. “Yeah, Vegas, it is.”

Chapter Five

Lyah

Lyah could've robbed him and took his car had she wanted. But if she wasn't sure karma would bite her in the ass for repaying him back that way for technically saving her life twice, she would've dared to. Not to mention she was shocked when he offered his clothes to her. He didn't have to do that.

He was growing on her: snippy ways and all.

Besides, she really wanted to see what Las Vegas was all about. She might even find out who this Tally person was. Her curiosity was peaked from the text messages she had seen on his phone about calling him back. Apparently, she was making a big mistake.

Was he trying to stop a wedding? Lyah didn't peg him as the type to just drive cross-country to a wedding to stop it. But then again, he probably never pegged himself as someone to pick up a stranger and go to Vegas with them either.

Lyah lay in bed as the sun peaked through curtains by Keith's bed. He hadn't yet awakened, though it was pushing past 10 a.m. She wondered if they would hang back before hitting the road again. Checkout wasn't for another hour.

She turned to look at him again, as she found herself unable to stop accessing him continuously when she awoke hours ago. The sun was hitting his golden-brown hair just right to cast a golden halo on his head. He slept with his mouth slightly open, and—yes, he did snore, though not loudly. Without his glasses perched on his face, he had the perfect boy-next-door look.

He was cute in a goody-two-shoe, grumpy, nerdy way.

Keith stirred and slowly opened his eyes, his eyes landing on her smiling ones. He jumped back in surprise and looked at the clock beside the bed. "Why are you staring at me while I sleep? That's creepy."

"You snore," Lyah grinned.

Keith frowned. "No, I don't."

Lyah nodded her head. "Yeah, you do. And it's loud. You should work on that. Maybe buy something for your sinuses."

She was lying, but the puzzled look on his face as he tried to remember if he did nor not was priceless. She stretched as she pulled the covers away from her legs.

Keith turned away abashed. "Why didn't you wear the sweat-pants I gave you?"

Lyah looked down at the oversized shirt and boxers that he gave her. She liked to sleep light due to getting hot easily at night. The sweatpants still lied on the back of the chair, where she left it after her shower.

"I enjoyed this better. Why? Are my legs making you uncomfortable?" she teased.

Still turned away, he said, "Are you not afraid of being exposed to a complete stranger?"

Lyah waved him off. "Is this about last night? You're harmless, Keith. That I know. This is way more modest than my dress."

Keith whipped his head to her, a deep shade across his cheeks. "How do you know? How do you know I'm not harmless?"

"Because if you wanted something from me, you would've tried it already, like most do."

Most of the guys she met on the road tried to get in her pants within an hour of meeting her. Keith didn't even look like he belonged outside of college. He had manners, though he tried to pretend he didn't. Lyah was weary about judging a book by their cover, though, if her last encounter was anything to go by. But she had a good feeling about Keith, and she trusted her gut.

"Whatever. We leave soon. I'm not spending another night here."

"Ditto."

They cleaned up and took turns in the bathroom, Keith changing into a pair of jeans and a green sweatshirt before brushing his teeth. Lyah had to improvise with the teeth brushing as she had no toothbrush. Instead of asking for another pair of clothes, she chose to wear the gray sweatpants she had refused before bed and kept the black t-shirt on. The jacket still remained in her possession. Her hair, now wet and curled due to her raking it with her fingers in the bathroom, sat at the base of her neck in an improvised bun.

She stuffed her bra and panties into her pocket, noting that she would have to buy another pair when they got to a store. She followed Keith's lead as he checked out from the motel and made his way to the car, placing his duffle bag back in the truck along with Lyah's dress.

"Are we going to stop for something to eat? Like real food?" Lyah asked carefully. Her stomach growled as if to reiterate her point.

"I'll see if we can run through a drive-thru along the way," he answered as he hopped in the car.

Lyah didn't argue. They were past the point of snacks; she was sure he was rather hungry himself.

Hopping back on the highway, they traveled less than two miles before exiting to line up at a McDonald's. The line was relatively long, given the morning run. It took a good minute before it was time to order. Lyah already knew what she wanted.

Keith was forced to open his door to talk, considering he could not remove the plastic from the window.

"*Welcome to McDonald's, can I take your order?*"

Keith turned to Lyah. "What do you want?"

"Four McGriddles, a hash brown, and a medium orange juice."

Keith stared at her in disbelief. "You're going to eat all that?"

Lyah gave him a pointed look. "You'd be surprised what I can fit down my throat."

She hadn't meant for it come off as innuendo, but she was too hungry to correct her tone or care. The look on Keith's face was nothing short of amusing.

He recited her order and added his—two sausage biscuits and a hash brown with a French Vanilla Frappuccino. By the time he pulled up to the window, Lyah felt like she was dying for hunger.

He passed her bag and drink to her as he paid for both of their food. He parked under a tree, and they both indulged in the delight of hot food. It wasn't until Lyah was on her third McGriddle did she realize that he had willingly paid for her food even with the knowledge that she had cash.

"Thank you," she muffled as she shuffled the hot food in her mouth.

Keith finished chewing his food before asking, "For what?"

"The food. For paying for it. I'll give you back the cash."

Keith shrugged as if it were nothing. "Don't worry about it. Save your money for the clothes."

Pity he didn't know she still had well over $2000 in her possession. But what he didn't know wouldn't hurt him.

"When are we stopping for some clothes?"

"Let's just see how far we can drive first, and then we'll stop at a shop somewhere close."

It sounded like a good plan. They were back on the road before she knew it. It was a lovely day for a cross-country adventure, like one of those days that she'd watch on TV. Not a cloud was in the sky.

Surprisingly, the radio was still on the station she had left it. An unrecognizable slow tune seeped through the speakers, creating a sense of calm and comfort she hadn't felt before.

"Did you really mean it?" Keith asked.

Lyah turned to him, confused by his question. "Mean what?"

"You really don't have any family? Or friends?"

It wasn't a lie, though the way he said it made it sound like he believed them to be dead. It was more so she had no home to go to because she wasn't welcomed. The only "friend" she had left to live his life two years ago.

"In a sense, yes."

Keith nodded as if he were digesting the information. Lyah didn't elaborate further. He sensed her hesitation, so he decided to change the subject.

"So, where are you from?"

"Originally, from New Jersey. I moved a lot as a kid but eventually, we settled in Connecticut. I'm just going with the flow these days," Lyah answered.

Keith held a pensive look on his face like he was battling whether to ask his next question. "So, are you… homeless?"

In hindsight, she was. Lyah never stayed in a motel for more than a week. She opted to hop around New England as often as possible. But the word bothered her more than she thought it would. There was an edge to her voice, and it dripped with bitterness from the memories of leaving home. "I'm not homeless. I just… I just move around a lot. That's all."

Keith didn't seem to take offense to her tone. "How long have you been… moving around?"

Since sneaking out of her mother's place two years ago, she hadn't stopped moving nor had she looked back. Initially, it was because she didn't want anyone to find her. Eventually, she started to like it. Plus, it helped that she was never stable when it came to her targets. No one ever knew who she was.

Now, though, things felt different. Lyah wasn't sure why or how, but it did.

"For a while," Lyah eventually answered.

"And you're not scared out there by yourself? Especially after what just happened?"

It was weird seeing the concern in his eye. She had only seen irritation and anger since meeting him. This new look almost made her want to spill her guts, but she refrained.

"I'm not scared of anything," Lyah said, putting on a brave face.

Though it was a total lie. Everyone was scared of something. It scared her to take things from people not knowing what they were capable of, especially with the last incident. It frightened her that she'd probably never find stability and likely die on the streets.

She had nothing and probably never would.

Keith shook his head, dismissing that notion. "I don't believe that. You have to be scared of something. Hell, everyone is."

"Then, what are you afraid of?"

"Where do I even start?"

Lyah turned in her seat to face him. "Are *you* scared of being out here? Being with me? Maybe driving to Las Vegas to see Tally?"

Keith whipped his head to her. "How do you know about Tally?"

Lyah shrugged. "From the text messages you sent her, it wasn't hard to put two-and-two together. I never pegged you for the romantic type."

He was quiet for a moment before he answered, "Things changed. I changed."

"How?"

"I just realized that I have to start doing things for me and not because it was dictated to me."

"So, you want control over your life?" Lyah got that. It was the reason she left home in the first place.

Keith nodded. "And going after what I really want."

"Starting with Tally?"

"Starting with Tally," he confirmed.

"But what if it doesn't work out? How do you know this is what she wants?"

Keith got a sour look on his face. "Because nobody falls in love and marries that fast. We've been over barely six months. There's just no way. We have history."

Lyah wanted to tell him that almost anything is possible when it came to love. She heard of people getting married after a week of meeting and living happily ever after. Sometimes it wasn't about history. It was about connection.

But he seemed determined, and she couldn't knock him for trying. He needed this journey to see for himself. So, she didn't discourage it.

"Do what makes you happy," she encouraged.

"I plan on it."

Chapter Six

Keith

Keith hadn't meant to spill his guts to Lyah, but it was nice to have someone listen. In fact, if he hadn't caught himself, he likely would've told her the whole story of his relationship with Tally.

It was strange how easy it was to get lost in the short tale. He tried to remember Lyah was still practically a stranger. Perhaps stranger wasn't the correct term, but, she was far from a friend.

A road trip buddy, maybe?

Keith shook his head, deciding to tackle that thought later. It was nearing evening, and they still hadn't made it across Ohio due to heavy traffic on the Interstate. For the most part, Lyah had busied herself with snacking and doing crossword puzzles from his crossword book she found in his back seat.

He wouldn't go as far as saying he enjoyed her company, but he felt comfortable enough to ease into their drive. Maybe she was growing on him. He stole a look in her direction for what felt like the hundredth time.

Though it bothered him at first, he liked the way his clothes fit on her. It was baggy and long, but it made her look—dare he say—cute with her petite frame. She had a line of light freckles that peppered her make-up free face, and her button nose almost made her look innocent.

Almost.

Nevertheless, she was going to need her own clothes and soon. Keith spied a sign about a thrift store some miles back, and the exit was approaching. It was better to do their shopping now than later before night came since he wasn't planning to stop any time after.

Without explanation, Keith took the exit, which caused her to look up from the crossword book. "Where are we going?"

"To do that shopping we promised. There's a thrift store not too far from here."

He pulled into the mostly empty parking lot before sunset. The store wasn't hard to miss below the overpass after he exited the Interstate. It didn't take them long before they were inside.

The store was considerably big in that it housed not only clothes but furniture and books alike in the back. A few straggling shoppers zig-zagged around them as they stood in the middle of the floor, wondering where to begin.

"I guess I'll head this way and meet back with you when I'm done," Lyah said, pointing to the women's section to the left of the store.

"Sounds like a plan."

They split up after that, Keith finding himself engulfed in the men's section while Lyah disappeared between some clothing racks. He figured he should get a few items for himself considering the slight change in plans, and he wasn't sure when they would reach Las Vegas. It was already taking longer than he expected due to his run-in with Lyah. He should've been cruising through Illinois by now.

Nevertheless, he picked up a few outfits to add to his duffel bag and a pair of flip-flops since he knew he wasn't likely to get his old ones back from Lyah, even if she bought shoes. He was about to head back with his few items to wait for her at their intended spot when he spied her peering into a jewelry glass. A few clothes were draped on her arm, and a pair of tennis shoes danged from her fingers.

She was so fascinated by what was inside, she hadn't noticed the bald man staring at her from a few feet away across the glass. Dressed in all black with boots, his face hard and focused, the man looked exactly like someone to stay away from.

Keith frowned as he slowly approached Lyah, more so out of concern than curiosity at what she was staring at in the glass casing. His eyes unwavering, the man opened his black coat and pulled out a phone. He tapped something on his screen, finally averting his eyes but not before slicing Keith with a cold glance, as if telling him he knew he was there the whole time. The man placed a hand on his hip and held it there like a warning. Like he was reaching for something.

Keith stilled a moment causing him to pivot, his stomach lurched with unease. Who was this man?

But his question wouldn't find an answer anytime soon as the man suddenly turned at his heel and disappeared outside the store shortly after. Lyah hadn't noticed a thing.

Keith felt the air finally seep back into his body as he found movement in his legs again to reach Lyah. Putting the strange man out his thoughts, he surveyed the glass container.

The jewelry piece Lyah was seemingly hypnotized by was a 14-carat gold ruby princess-cut diamond ring on display. It was a simple yet beautiful ring. However, the price tag on it was more aligned with a high-end jewelry store like Tiffany's.

Tally would've liked something like that, Keith thought. She had always been a jewelry freak with an expensive taste.

"That's a beautiful ring. A ring we cannot afford," Keith made a point to emphasize the last sentence.

Lyah turned to him with a "duh" expression. "I know that. Can't a girl admire in peace?"

If he wasn't worried she would steal it, he would've left her be. He ignored her question to look at the items in her hand. "More dresses? It's going to get cold in a few days. Wouldn't you prefer pants? Maybe your own jacket?"

Judging from her frown, she didn't appreciate his assessment. "Dresses make me feel more comfortable. Besides, what am I going to wear in Vegas? I can't walk around in sweats."

"Yeah, if you're walking through the Red-Light District. We're not going to party. Or at least I'm not." Honestly, he had no clue what she planned to do in Vegas once he dropped her off, and frankly, it wasn't his business, but the thought of her going back to her ways only brought a bad feeling.

Keith shook the thought from his head, not wanting to go there.

"The dresses stay. However, since you're so worried about my legs freezing, I'll get a few more stuff, Dad," she added as she skipped back to the ladies' section.

Keith rolled his eyes and decided to wait in line for checkout. He wasn't going to pay for her items as he figured she had money—*stolen* money, though he didn't know how much. The less he knew about Lyah's habits, the better.

His mind crept back to the man he saw earlier as he waited his turn. It was like the man was a shadow, gone in an instant. Did he know Lyah? Had she stolen from him, too? Keith knew traveling with her was risky, considering how they met. Was that guy from the motel still after them? He shuttered at the thought.

By the time Keith made it to the cashier, Lyah had side-stepped the few old ladies waiting behind him to toggle her items with his. One passed them a dirty look.

"What are you doing?" Keith asked, a little annoyed. He took in the red beret on her head and the black scarf around her neck.

Lyah posed, throwing one end of the scarf over her shoulder. "You like? I feel like a French girl. *Je suis fabulous!*"

"I'm pretty sure that's not how you pronounce 'fabulous' in

French."

Lyah waved him off. The young female cashier took note of Lyah's clothes thrown next to his. "Together or separate?"

"Together."

"Separate." They said at the same time.

Keith and Lyah turned to each other simultaneously. "I'm not paying for your stuff," Keith proclaimed.

"Who said anything about you paying?"

The cashier looked between the two before asking, "So… together?"

"No."

"Yes." They said simultaneously.

"Seriously, Lyah, can we not do this right now?"

"What am I doing?" She seemed genuinely confused.

Keith felt like he wanted to rip his hair out in aggravation. "Whatever it is you're doing right now!"

Lyah turned to him, her eyes hard. "I don't think you're paying attention, Keith. I'm not asking you to pay." She gestured to the cashier to ring everything up.

It dawned on him what she meant. "I'm not letting *you* pay for my stuff."

"I wasn't asking," Lyah emphasized.

Keith could only watch in defeat as both of their stuff was placed in shopping bags and handed to them. When it came time to pay, Keith was shocked—and not so shocked—to see Lyah pull out a wad of cash from her—his—pocket.

She counted out an even $200 to give to the cashier and all but shoved her bags in Keith's already full hands. "I paid you back for lunch. Now you pay me back for the clothes by bringing them to the car."

"First of all, that wasn't the deal. Second, demanding much?" Keith said, though he still followed her to the car with both their bags in hand. Unconsciously, he kept an eye out for the man he saw earlier, sweeping over the few vehicles still in the parking lot.

Lyah walked backward to look at him and shrugged, no clue as to Keith's silent inquiry. "It's the Artisan way or nothing."

"Artisan?" Keith asked as he dropped the bags in the trunk of the wagon.

Lyah visibly hesitated. He wondered if she had meant to say that.

"My last name."

They got into the car and soon zipped out the parking lot and back to the Interstate. "So, Lyah Artisan?"

She nodded. "That's the name, don't wear it out."

"Interesting," Keith uttered. With her last name, it was like he could put together a mockup of the person that had invaded his space over the last 36 hours.

"What's your last name?"

Keith shook his head. "I wasn't offering."

Lyah pouted. "Please?"

Keith stayed quiet, hoping she got the message.

"You realize I could just grab your wallet from your pocket and find out for myself?"

The idea of her hand rummaging through his pockets while he drove strangely made him buzz with a new feeling. Not wanting her anywhere near him, he answered, "Fine. It's Hayden."

Lyah stared at him in deep thought. "You look more like a Stevenson."

"How the hell can I look like another name?"

"I don't know. I guess I always associated 'Steve' with nerds."

Keith gapped at her. "Nerd? You think I'm a nerd?"

Lyah threw on an innocent face. "Well, yeah. You have the, 'I'm preppy and smart, and my parents do everything for me' look."

She wasn't too far off, though it only served to piss him off. He stewed in his seat.

"I am not preppy, and I'll have you know, I am very independent!"

"Your Princeton sweater says otherwise. On top of that, I've seen the number of times your parents called you. Is that why you turned it off? Are they mad their little scholar has run off?"

It was scary how observant she was. Keith quickly tried to think of a rebuttal, but considering how little he knew of her, he felt better fighting fire with a cold shoulder.

"Fuck off, Lyah. You don't know anything about me."

Taken aback by his abrasive tone, she remained quiet to Keith's relief as they drove for miles until the sun had disappeared entirely across the horizon. Finally, they made it out of Ohio and into Indiana when Keith could feel his vision began to blur from fatigue.

He wanted to get as far as possible for the night. Though he still had time before Tally would be crossing the threshold, he wanted to get there as soon as possible before he completely lost his nerve.

He jerked his head up when he realized he was drooping, drawing Lyah's attention. "What's wrong with you? Are you tired?"

"I'm fine," he said a bit snippier than intended.

Lyah frowned. "You don't look fine. You look like you're ready to pass out. Can you even see to drive?"

"I said I'm fine, Lyah."

Lyah couldn't accept his answer, much to his chagrin. "Keith, if you're tired, just let me drive. I don't have a wink of sleep in me."

Keith shook his head, gripping the stirring wheel a little tighter as his eyes blurred in and out. "You're not driving my car. Besides, do you even have a license?"

He knew she didn't because she barely carried anything on her. "That's irrelevant. I can drive, that's all that matters."

"Irrelevant?" he almost screeched.

"Just let me help. It's either that or you get us both killed by falling asleep at the wheel."

"No. I said I'm fine!"

Suddenly, he made a move to switch lanes but jerked it back, Keith not seeing the car in his blind spot. A horn blared as the car sped past him, a finger pressed against the glass of the passenger's side of the car. He carefully merged onto the emergency lane soon after, and he breathed a sigh of relief once he parked.

Lyah sat with a hand tightly wound on the door handle. With an exhausted sigh, he started, “Ok. Maybe you’re right. I’m tired. I’ll let you drive but on a few conditions.”

Lyah scoffed as she crossed her arms. “These better not be stupid conditions.”

Keith ignored her comment. “Number one: no stopping. I’ll only need an hour or two of sleep, and then you can wake me to drive the rest of the way. Number two: no detours. We have snacks in the back if you’re hungry and if you need the bathroom, hold it.”

“As if—”

“Number three: be gentle with the car, *please*.”

“I think we’re a little past gentle, don’t you think? I mean, it’s a station wagon for Christ’s sakes. Not to mention your window is basically nonexistent.”

“Are we clear?” Keith asked.

Lyah rolled her eyes but agreed. “Yes.”

Satisfied, Keith nodded and looked through the rearview mirror. There were many cars zipping past at ungodly speed, and the shoulder lane wasn’t the widest. If he opened his door, he’d risk getting clipped, and the railing on the other side made it hard to open the passenger door.

Lyah seemed to be thinking what he thought because she perked, “Maybe we can just slide over.”

Keith thought for a moment, but he knew it was the only option. "Fine. Let's get this over with."

They both scooted over to each other as there was no middle console. "I guess I'll just go over," Lyah muttered as she eased up and over Keith, her body brushing his as he scooted to the passenger side. He caught a whiff of her pumpkin scent as she had passed. It was just like the shampoo from the motel. Keith cleared his throat, which suddenly felt dry.

Keith ignored the flare of heat that burned his skin as he made himself comfortable. "You can adjust the seat if you like."

"I plan to," she replied as she made the necessary adjustments. Finally, she prepared herself to ease into traffic.

"Do you know where to go?"

"We got GPS, don't we? Besides, I've been to the west, just not Vegas. I can handle it."

"Remember, 1-2 hours. Don't forget to wake me."

"Aye-aye, Captain."

Though apprehensive at first, it didn't take long for Keith to drift into slumber as he thought about how soft her skin had felt when it brushed his as she maneuvered across his lap. He chanted Tally's name in his mind like a prayer, but it didn't ease his awareness.

God help him, his thoughts were sure to be plagued by sinful dreams he would dread later.

Chapter Seven

Lyah

Keith jolted awake when his head slammed against the window. With his hand to his temple, he turned to Lyah, now bright-eyed and awake.

"What the hell is going on?"

Lyah turned to him with panic in her eyes. She flittered between him and the rearview mirror. Her speed continued to increase as she spoke. "We're being followed, and they just slammed into us!"

Keith turned back, but the headlights of the truck blinded them both. "Who are 'they?'"

"If I knew, I would've told you!"

Lyah swerved out of the way as the truck sped up to hit them again. "It could be the guy from the motel. You just had to steal from him!"

Even in a panic, he found a way to be condescending. "How? There's no way he'd catch up with us that fast!"

They braced in their seats as the truck hit them again, this time making a hard impact. Keith's face hit the dashboard, causing a trail of blood to trickle down his temple. Lyah was lucky enough not to get hit.

"Pull off the side of the road!"

"I can't! There's nowhere to go! I've got cars on both sides."

"Then, speed up!"

Lyah floored it as the truck swung side-to-side behind them, the headlights illuminating them bright as day. If any other car was concerned, they certainly had left them in their lane. A sign for the next exit offered some hope for Lyah as she did her best to outpace the truck, though it wouldn't last very long in the station wagon.

"There's an exit coming. Maybe we can outrun the truck on the regular road!" Lyah offered Keith as he squeezed the door handle.

"Highly doubt it, but it's the best we got!"

Before the truck could ram them again, Lyah swerved to the right at the last minute to get out of the line of impact from the truck, which couldn't turn at the last minute.

"Yes!" she exclaimed as she sped through the exit.

Keith looked as if he wasn't sure whether to cry or be relieved. "You did it! You actually did it!"

Lyah turned to him with excitement, "Don't ever doubt me again! I don't know what that was, but I was the one who saved—"

"Lyah, watch out!"

Lyah turned back to the road, completely forgetting she was driving on the regular road, and swerved out of the lane to avoid hitting a lone car at the stoplight. In shock, she failed to press the brakes but instead accelerated through the red light, causing a yell from her and Keith as the car clipped a curb and careened them down an embankment as Lyah struggled to regain control.

The rushing noise of metal bending and the violent whipping of air came to a crashing halt as a deafening silence sliced through them. A painful throb and burning feeling overtook Lyah's body as she tried to wiggle from her position, not realizing the car was sandwiched between two trees in a forested area.

She craned her neck to see how Keith was faring, but he was completely knocked out. In a panic, she reached over to him to check his pulse, a sigh of relief releasing from her lips as she felt the hot air from under his nose.

"Shit!" she mumbled to herself. How could she be so stupid? When the truck first started tailing her, she had signaled for them to go around. Then they had started getting aggressive, and Lyah being Lyah, toyed with them by braking. They hadn't liked that.

Still, the question lingered: was this her target's bidding? She couldn't see how it would've been possible. They were so far from him, and as far as she knew, he didn't have a vehicle. Maybe he knew where they were going and had friends tail them? But why not attack sooner? If this incident was random, then she'd chalk it up to her bad luck, but her gut was saying otherwise. And her gut feeling never lied. Not to mention, initially she did nothing on the road to warrant that reaction from a stranger.

Lyah cradled her head as she looked around to assess the damage. The backseat of the wagon was caved in, the windows were blown out, the driver side plastic tore, and the bits of branches somehow sat in the back seat. If they had been sitting back there, things would've been much worse.

If Keith's father would've been angry about the window, she could only imagine how he'd react, knowing how it looked now. He'd probably have a heart attack.

Lyah looked over to Keith again, noting his bruised lip and the blood from his hairline. She reached over and shook him.

"Keith? Keith?"

He didn't move or offer any indication of hearing her. She tried shaking him a little harder, though she made sure not to overdo it as she didn't know the extent of his injuries.

"Keith!"

He groaned and slowly opened his eyes, taking a sharp breath as he struggled to lean back in the seat. Lyah breathed a sigh of relief, a hand over her chest. "Lyah? Where are we?" His voice sounded scratchy like he'd just awaken from a nap. Well, technically…

"I don't know. We hit a curb and flew through a forested area, I think. We're lucky to be alive."

Keith turned to her with anger in his eyes, though he winced at the tension. "Yeah, no thanks to you. Dammit, my dad is going to strangle me," he murmured the last bit to himself, his voice conflicted.

Lyah wanted to retort, but she knew he was right. If she hadn't gotten them in this mess, they'd likely be on their merry way by now.

"Are you hurt?" she asked, genuinely concerned. Keith appeared to have minor injuries, but he could be hurting internally.

"I'm fine."

She noted he didn't ask if she was okay, but it wasn't the time to dwell.

"We need to get out of here. It's only a matter of time before that truck finds the skid marks on the pavement and find out we're still in the area, that is if it is who we think it is." Lyah suggested.

"Agreed."

They took off their seatbelts and tried to find a way out of the car. Lyah contemplated climbing out the window as the doors wouldn't jimmy open.

"Shit."

"What?" Keith asked.

"My door isn't opening. Yours?"

Keith pushed his door with his shoulder but groaned in pain when it didn't budge. "It's jammed."

"Looks like the window it is," Lyah muttered to herself as she attempted to crawl through the plastic-covered window. However, she didn't get very far as a sharp pain pierced her abdomen, causing her to fall back into her seat.

"Ow!" she exclaimed as she grabbed the spot.

"What is it?"

Lyah lifted her shirt to assess her wound. There was a deep gash against her stomach, her skin raw and bloody surrounding the area. Her shirt was wet with blood, something she hadn't considered earlier. Why hadn't she felt it before? Lyah looked to the ripped plastic around the window frame. Perhaps moving wasn't the best idea.

"That doesn't look too good. Are you okay?" Concern dripped through his voice. His edge from earlier had dissipated.

Was she? A throb began to creep against her temples, and suddenly she could hear the rush of blood in her ears.

"I-I'm fine," she struggled to say. "We need to get out of here, like, right now."

"But—"

She didn't let him finish. Instead, she pushed off and proceeded to crawl out. She bit the stinging hiss that threatened to leave her mouth as she fell into a bush the car had ended up over with an *oof.*

Keith was right behind her, landing in her spot after she rolled over to the side. "Ow! I think I got glass in my hand," he hissed as he looked to his hand. A thin trail of blood trickled down his palm.

Lyah was about to say something smart, but the throb on her abdomen began to grow. She remained quiet as Keith helped her to her feet. "What now?" she asked.

Keith sighed, shaking his head as he looked at his totaled wagon. "My dad is going to kill me…" he trailed off. "We gotta get the car out of here. We should call…"

He patted his pockets, then turned to Lyah in alarm. "Where's my phone?"

"I don't know."

"Shit," he murmured frantically as he leaned in from the broken window to search for his phone, careful not the touch the broken glass pieces and reinjure himself. "Crap!"

"What is it?" Lyah painfully inched closer to him. In his palm was his phone, though it didn't look much like one. The screen was smashed like a hammer had taken to it. "Did you try turning it on? It might still work. People have cracked screens all the time."

Cracked. Not smashed.

"I'm trying," he said in frustration. "It's no use. How are we going to call for help?"

Lyah would've suggested they walk back to the street, but with the truck possibly in the area, they might end up worse than they were. So, she came up with a better idea. At least, to her, it was.

"Let's walk through the woods."

Keith turned to her like she was crazy. "Walk through the woods? We don't even know where we are! Where does it ever end?"

"It's either that or we take our chances with the truck that was following us. If they knew how to find us the first time, I highly doubt it would take them long to see us walking the streets. Not to mention we can't call for a ride, and there's barely anyone on the street this late to hail a taxi."

Keith stood quiet for a moment contemplating her words. "Where do we even start? And what about the stuff in the car?"

Lyah struggled to not limp as she made her way over to the trunk, a shot of pain hitting her right leg. Though the car was totaled, the trunk was in better repair than the rest of the body. The duffel bag he carried was still intact, including the clothes they bought. They could easily take them. She pulled them out through mangled metal and handed them to him.

"This should carry us for a while with whatever snacks and drinks we can scrimmage from the back."

"A while? How long is a while? Snacks can't hold us."

"It will until our next stop."

"We're going to need more food and water and a place to stay. God knows how long we'll have to walk, and what about the car? I can't just leave it here—"

Lyah grabbed him by the shoulders. He wasn't getting it. If they were in as much danger as her gut told her they were in, he needed to get it together and fast. She had never seen him so unhinged before. Staring right into his hazel eyes, she reassured, "It's going to be fine, Keith. We'll get through the woods; we'll get far away from this place. We'll figure out the car situation, everything. It'll work out, I promise."

She meant every word. She led them both into this mess; she'd get them out, too.

He didn't say anything to her, though he continued to stare at her as if he was trying to figure something out. Feeling a little exposed for lack of a better term, she removed her hands and stepped back, taking one of the shopping bags from his full hands.

"We should try to get as much as possible from the car. At the next stop, maybe we can call the police if they're not already on their way or a tow truck. Honestly, it's your call."

He never responded though he did join her in rummaging the car for whatever they could find that they needed or could carry. She discovered their snacks scattered around the interior, a few busted open, but surprisingly, her liquor was still intact.

"Of all the things..." she mumbled as she kissed the bottle and placed it in her bag.

"I think that's it. We'll have to come back for the rest or call a tow truck when we find a place."

Lyah was a little shocked. "No police?"

Keith shrugged. "What's the point? The truck is gone, or so we think, and there's no evidence to back up the theory that it's the guy from the motel. We might even get cited or arrested if they find out you were driving, and to make matters worse, the car is still in my dad's name. They'll call him about it. I'd rather take my chances in the woods. I'll figure it out another time."

He started walking ahead of her with Lyah struggling to catch up. The sharp pain in her abdomen was increasing, though she didn't want to say anything. She could only hope it wasn't anything serious.

The woods were dense and patchy. A clearing here, a clearing there, but no real sense of direction. If it wasn't for the moon, they would've likely been doomed.

Keith hadn't said a word since they began their journey. She wasn't sure whether that was a good thing or not. He had seemed so worried earlier, but now he was so silent, pensive almost. She wondered if he was in shock. And what was with that look earlier?

Lyah still couldn't decipher what that look was about. It was like he was trying to figure something out but couldn't say it.

Either way, Lyah pressed on behind him as she adjusted the bags in her hand for the umpteenth time. Maybe carrying their shopping bags wasn't the best idea, she thought.

"I think I see something," Keith quipped as he slowed to a stop.

"What is it?"

"I don't know… A cabin, maybe?"

Lyah highly doubted it, given the area and proximity to the Interstate. "Maybe it's a small ranch?"

"Whatever it is, we need to get there ASAP."

With a bit more urgency in their step, they stalked over to the place. As they inched closer, Lyah realized she was right. Empty land surrounded the property in an equestrian styled ranch. A small barn stood off to the side, though the doors were closed with no way to see inside.

The ranch didn't look in tip-top shape, but that was expected in the middle of nowhere. It was a wooden two-story structure that looked as if it would fall apart any day. The brown shutters sat half-hanging near the dirtied windows, there was a noticeable hole through one of the second-story windows, and the smell of animal was prominent.

The only nice thing about the property was the shaved grassland.

"Do we knock on the door?" Keith asked.

Lyah thought for a moment. Complete with how they looked, what time of the morning it was, and their sudden appearance in the middle of nowhere, they were likely to get the police called or worse, shot.

"I don't think that's a good idea."

Keith turned to her, puzzled. "Why not? This is a perfect opportunity to get rest or even a good meal. Maybe even heal properly." His eyes flittered to her abdomen.

"We don't know who or what is in there. For all we know, it's an enthusiastic triggerman waiting for the opportunity for two random strangers covered in blood and appearing out of nowhere to knock on their door. Look at us! Would you open the door for you or me at four in the morning?"

Keith looked dejected. "No… So, what do we do now?"

Lyah considered the barn. She pointed to it, saying, "Maybe we stakeout? Stay in the barn until they leave, take what we need and be our way."

"Wait, wait, wait… you want us to break into the house? We're better off just knocking on the door!"

"In what world would that end well, huh? Just trust me on this." Lyah began stalking for the barn, leaving Keith to reluctantly follow behind. Getting closer, they could hear the wails of a horse over the deep-throated crickets of the night. As they inched closer, they searched their surroundings to make sure the area was clear.

The barn doors were big and bulky, but they cracked it open together and slipped through. The stable only had two horses inside but about four lambs walking about. Plenty of hay was stacked in corners and in the chambers, and the stable was well lit.

Keith looked around in disgust. “I can’t believe we’re doing this. It smells awful in here.”

“Well, believe it, college kid. We got a long night ahead of us, and the stench is here to stay.”

Lyah steered them to an empty chamber with lots of hay. “This is where we’ll camp out for tonight. It’s hidden enough, so in case someone does come in, we can have time to escape.”

Keith dropped the items from his hands to the ground. “You say camp like this is supposed to be a fun experience.”

Lyah also dropped her belongings. “Some people would call this thrilling.”

“Good thing I’m not ‘some people.’”

Lyah spread the jacket in her hand on the hay for the both of them and tried to sit. She winced and clutched her abdomen as she tried to get comfortable. Keith was still in his own world, scrutinizing the barn before joining her on the hay.

He blew out a breath before turning to her. “How’s the injury?”

“It’s getting better,” Lyah lied. The pain was borderline unbearable, but he didn’t need to know that. “I’ll survive. How are you doing? You took a pretty nasty hit, too. I wouldn’t be surprised if you have a concussion."

Keith shrugged and looked away. "That's the least of my worry. I just hope I make it out of here alive to go see Tally. I only have a few days left."

Lyah grabbed his shoulder reassuringly. "We'll get there, I promise."

"Yeah," was the only thing he replied before turning his back to her and snuggling into himself. Lyah stared up at the blinding light, wondering what the next few days had in store for them. She only hoped they could make it out alive.

Chapter Eight

Keith

Keith blinked a few times before realizing he had fallen asleep. Searching around, he spotted Lyah lying beside him, her body halfway off the hay. Her right leg was draped over his torso. How and when that happened, he wasn't sure. But he obviously found comfort in it as his hand was holding it steady. If anyone had walked in on them, they'd likely assume the two were dead by way of their position.

Out the corner of his eye, he could see a horse in the next stall staring straight at him in curiosity. The horse huffed and turned away from him as if disgusted by his existence.

Huh.

Keith shuffled to his feet haphazardly, pulling Lyah's leg off him and ultimately awakening her as well. Her discomfort and confusion marred her features as she clutched her stomach and straightened.

"God, it smells in here," she croaked.

"That's an understatement," Keith mumbled.

The commotion of Lyah falling back onto the hay caused him to turn and curse. She seemed dazed and out of it. It was then he noticed the blood soaking the shirt she had on. Even through the faded black shirt, the wet spot was visible.

"Did you bleed all night?"

Lyah rolled her eyes but hissed as she struggled to sit correctly. "If I did, I couldn't tell you. I'm sure it's nothing. We should start moving."

Keith knitted his eyebrows in concern. "Lyah, that isn't nothing. Your shirt is soaking! Maybe we should go to the hospital—"

"I'm not going to the hospital, Keith Please, just… I don't want to go, okay? I want to keep moving. This isn't my first injury. I know how to take care of it. Trust me."

Trust her? That was hard to do considering their predicament. She was stubborn when she wanted to be. Lyah was clearly in a lot of pain, and though he wasn't a health expert, he suspected that amount of blood loss couldn't be good.

"I know you think you got everything under control, Lyah, but this is not the time to play hero. You need help. At the very least, let me dress your wound. I'll go along with your plan and take what we need from the house, but you must let me help you. It won't do us any good if you're not up to speed."

"You don't look any better yourself. You're bruised and bloody, too."

"Yeah, but I'm not the one continuously hissing in pain while clutching my wounds."

Lyah looked defiant as if she were about to argue but decided against it. "If we're going through with the plan, I'm coming with you."

"You're not coming with me, Lyah—"

"You can't do this on your own. At least let me be your eyes. You've never broken into anything before. I can guide you."

Keith placed his hand on his hips. "How do you know I've never broken into anything? You don't know me."

"I can read you like a book, Keith," Lyah began. "You don't have a bad bone in your body."

"And you know this, how? Based on assumptions? My appearances? You know nothing about me and what I'm capable of doing."

"You're not a risk-taker. You complain and whine every chance you get. You've had your life handed to you! I can smell a spoon-feed baby from a mile away, and you are a stench."

Keith flinched. Where was this attitude coming from? His anger festered until his blood began to boil. If he were a cartoon character, he'd imagine steam flowing through his ears like a hot kettle. He tried to hold his tongue, but her comment had hurt him, more so because it was true. Though he knew better to engage as he was sure her pain and embarrassment were speaking for her, he couldn't help what came out of his mouth next.

"You know what, Lyah? You sure have a lot of talk for someone who has no direction and no allies. You have nothing to your name, and all you do is steal and leech off people. It doesn't take a genius to figure out that you've got nowhere to go in life. You think you're better because you know how to manipulate people and break into shit? News flash, it just makes you a criminal and a bitch! It's a wonder you haven't ended up in a ditch already!"

He regretted those words as soon as it left his mouth. He'd gone too far. Way too far. But Lyah struck a nerve, and he was tired of people acting like they knew him. Like they knew what was best for him. He's heard it from his parents, his brother, even Tally and his friends.

Tally.

It was like she had gotten lost in the whole ordeal of trying to find safety from ghosts. His plans had derailed from the start, and now he was in a nasty barn like a sitting duck. Was this punishment? If it wasn't, then it was now after he'd nearly bitten Lyah's head off for sticking to her guns.

Lyah sat quiet, a palpable tension drifting in the air. An apology was at the tip of his tongue, but he kept his mouth shut. Now wouldn't be the time. They needed to get out of the barn and soon.

But they couldn't stand there all day and avoid each other. Regardless, they needed to survive and get to their destination so they would never have to see each other ever again. A knot formed at the base of his stomach, but he ignored it.

He dared not to glance in her direction for fear of seeing… pain, maybe? Or maybe it was the feeling of regret that had rooted so far in his core he felt the need to release the contents of his stomach? Either way, he coward like he always did.

"I'll go alone. I'll get what you need, and we'll be on our way."

Keith paused for a moment, slightly wishing for a reaction. She nodded, her head bowed, mouth slack. He pushed on, creeping out of the barn and scurrying across the fields to the house.

It was likely close to seven in the morning as the horizon started to bruise with different hues of purples and oranges. The house was still, and nothing looked any different than how it did when they first arrived. The red pickup trunk they spotted on the way to the barn hadn't moved an inched. It was only a matter of time before someone came out to check the barn. He needed to do this quickly.

Lyah was right. He never had so much as broken a rule outside of him running off to find Tally and leaving school behind. His nerves were getting the best of him. He rubbed his sweaty palms together, trying to find comfort or defuse his sudden shaking problem. It didn't help. He was about to break into a house with no protection or help, and no idea why the hell he hadn't kept his mouth shut so he wouldn't have to do this alone.

But his mind went back to Lyah alone in the barn, clutching her wound with her blood-stained shirt. He didn't like how that sight bothered him. And despite what he said to her, it would trouble him to see her in any more pain.

Was he gaining a soft spot for her? Was it pity? They weren't friends, they were complete opposites, and she was nothing but trouble. And yet, he couldn't bring himself to think about how they would part when the time came.

His mind ran to the man in the store and wondered if he was after them. He had only gotten a glimpse of the truck that ran them off the road, and he could've sworn he'd seen it sitting outside the thrift store when they left.

Was that man after them? Was he working with the guy from the motel? Keith couldn't shake the feeling that the motel guy was involved, but he chalked it up to nerves. After all, there was no evidence of that being the case, nor had they seen or heard from him. Not to mention they were likely far out of his reach. Maybe the man at the thrift store had a bone to pick with Lyah.

That wouldn't be good for them either, considering how menacing he looked.

The front door to the house burst open, causing Keith to crouch further down between the shrubs he was hiding behind. A stocky middle-aged man in a plaid button-down, dirty jeans, and a trucker hat stepped out onto his porch. He scanned the area before heading to his truck and hopping in. He started it without hesitation and drove off the lot on an old beaten path with dust and dirt kicking up behind the wheels.

A sigh of relief escaped him, but Keith kept his guard. One obstacle was out of the way, but he certainly needed to proceed with caution. There may still be someone else in the house.

Kneeling, he checked each window around the house to see any movement or signs of life. When he didn't see any, he headed to the front door and jiggled the lock. Surprisingly, he found it to be open.

Interesting. Did the man not know to secure his house? Though, judging by how the house looked, no one was likely to dare step foot inside even with the door unlocked—well, besides himself.

The front door heavily groaned as Keith opened and shut it behind him. The inside was just as rundown as the surface. The faded green couch in the living room was on the verge of falling apart. The kitchen straight ahead had dishes piled high in the sink as if they had never been washed. A foul smell of dirty laundry and mold suffocated him as he gently made his way around to search for canned goods.

Keith was able to find a shopping bag to throw in a couple items like soup and bottled water. When he finished, he climbed the steep stairs searching for a bathroom for medical supplies, each step creaking as he tried to gouge any human noises.

After searching the three bedrooms near him, he was finally able to find the bathroom down the hall. Opening the cabinets, he found gauze, band-aids, alcohol, medical tape, and pain relievers to stuff into the bag. Finding some other items he thought he might need under the sink, he stuffed them in the bag, too.

The sound of the truck door slamming jilted Keith as realization dawned on him. The owner was home. Quickly, he tied the bag and hid behind the shower curtains. He waited with a shaky breath escaping his lips every few seconds. His anxiety increased tenfold as the front door opened, then slammed, and heavy footsteps grew closer, inching up the stairs.

The footsteps faded as if the owner was heading in the opposite direction. Taking a chance, Keith started out of the tub until the footsteps returned, growing near again. Carefully, he closed back the curtain and stood stiff when the footsteps stopped in front of the bathroom.

He held his breath as the owner entered and closed the door. Keith sent a silent prayer and repentance for his missteps in case he was caught behind the curtains. The sound of a zipper opening caught his attention, and disgust etched on his face.

What sounded like water spewing from a fountain, Keith did his best to think happy thoughts as he was subjected to stand idle. A groan of pleasure had Keith ready to bolt, but he stayed put knowing he needed to get through this.

To his relief, the toilet flushed, and the footsteps faded out the door. Keith wanted to vomit at the prospect of the owner, not even washing his hands. Carefully, he stuck his head through the curtains and stepped out with the bag tied around his wrist.

The coast was clear. Keith tiptoed out the bathroom, careful not to touch anything else, and into the hall, frantically looking around him in case of a sneak attack. Noise from downstairs indicated the owner was likely in the kitchen.

There was no way he would be leaving through the front door with the owner downstairs. Keith paused and thought for a moment about another escape route.

The window, perhaps?

Two stories up, he'd have one hell of a fall, but that was likely his only option. He scanned the dilapidated rooms for windows. Two were bolted shut, and one facing the property's back led to a thorn bush below. His only other option was the broken window to the front he spied when they arrived. It was risky considering it was in plain view, but he'd have to make it work.

He stepped through the clothes on the ground in the room, cautious of the creaking floorboards, he tried to open the window since the hole wasn't big for him to fit through. It was like it was glued shut, forcing Keith to muster as much strength as he could. Still, in pain from the accident, he tried to ignore the sting that shot through his arms.

The sound of the front door opening and closing made Keith jump from the front window, crouching to see where the owner was going.

"Shit," Keith spat as he watched the man walk towards the barn. He needed to get out now for Lyah's sake.

With every strength he had, Keith pushed the window open and scurried onto the lower roof, praying the man didn't turn around. When he entered the barn, Keith took his opportunity to slide off the roof near the truck. He landed wrong on his foot, resulting in a quiet yelp. He inspected it quickly, but it didn't appear to be broke, though he was sure the pain would linger.

Not a second later, the man came out with one of his horses on the field. Keith scurried behind the truck to hide. Lyah wasn't with the man, nor did he look distressed. Maybe Lyah was able to hide.

Good. He couldn't deal if she'd gotten caught.

Heart pumping and adrenaline coursing through his veins, Keith made a beeline to the barn doors. The man disappeared along the trail that led behind his house and into the forest beyond. Keith's ankle flared with pinpricks, but he ignored it as best he could. By the time Keith made it back to the stall where Lyah was lying on the hay, eyes closed, he was about ready to collapse with exhaustion. He regretted not taking up a sport in high school when he had the chance.

Keith dropped the bag with a huff, "I think I got everything we need. We have to do this quick and head out before the owner comes back."

When he got no answer, he looked to Lyah, who hadn't moved an inch. He frowned and approached her. Her eyes were closed, and she was still. In a panic, he shook her. "Lyah? Lyah!"

Still no answer. Keith started to shake her but then thought better of it. Trying not to be frantic, he checked her pulse to be sure. Thankfully, she was still breathing, though it was a bit labored. How long ago had she passed out while he was in the house? He picked her up and laid her flat on the ground.

She looked so peaceful and innocent when she wasn't awake. The color in her usually shaded cheeks was faded, and her skin was hot. Being around a sickly cousin all his life, he thankfully knew what to do around people who fainted. Keith assessed the imprint of blood on her shirt, noting the dark spot got bigger.

Hesitantly, he lifted her shirt to find the wound. It was a deep gash running along her navel to her left side. She had likely gotten cut by some metal or glass in the wreckage. Though deep, the wound didn't look untreatable but he wished they could check it out by a professional. Still, the amount of blood that had been released was concerning.

Perhaps she was anemic? Or her constant movement had caused it to continue forcing out fluids?

Either way, he needed to stop the bleeding. Grabbing the rubbing alcohol, some tissue, and gauze, Keith carefully cleaned around the wound and worked his way to the center. It was inflamed and bruised, and the cut was a few centimeters longs. He could only hope that it wasn't more severe than it looked.

Keith was no medical expert, but he was determined to get the job done with what he had. He winced as he dabbed alcohol on her cut, careful not to waste too much. If she were awake, she likely would've screamed with pain. Lyah would feel it later when she awoke.

After he cleaned it, he used the gauze to wrap it and pulled her shirt back down. She hadn't stirred one bit, not even a flinch since he returned. He wondered if he was doing the right thing. Should he try to wake her again or let her rest? Maybe she had a concussion or something worse…

Keith decided not to dwell on negative thoughts. Lyah was strong, and she would be okay, he'd see to it. But they still needed to get out of the barn before the man came back from the trail. Leaving Lyah lying on the ground, he gathered their belongings, stuffing everything he could into one bag, and placed it near her. He needed to stake out the fields to make it to the truck.

It irked him, the idea of stealing someone's property. He had his argument ready for Lyah about not doing so, hoping they could walk instead. But considering her condition and their time limit on his end, he needed to do this. Consequences be damned.

With discretion, Keith crept alongside the barn walls to the entrance, peeking out to ensure no one was around. The coast was clear, and with that, he went back for their bag and dashed out, hiding the duffel in the bed of the truck. He then rushed back to the barn to gather Lyah. When he got back to the stall, she was finally starting to come to.

Thank God, he thought.

She squinted due to the bright light above. "Where am I?" she croaked.

Keith knelt beside her to pick her up. There was no time for explanations. "Just hold onto me for a sec. I'll explain everything once we're out of here."

Lyah, though weak, wrapped her arms around his neck and smothered her face into his shirt, no questions asked. His heart rate picked up, but it was likely from the adrenaline pumping his veins. At least, that's what he told himself. He made his way to the exit but stopped halfway when he heard shuffling outside the door.

Keith quickly dashed into one of the stalls that held another horse and hid behind a stack of hay. Lyah was still in his arms, eyes closed, and likely passed out again. He checked her pulse again just be sure. When he was satisfied, he turned his attention back to the barn doors.

The man walked past their stall with the horse in tow to the back of the barn. The other animals began to rile when he started getting their food ready on the barn's opposite side. Keith took that opportunity to inch closer to the barn exit, waiting until the owner turned his back. He didn't waste a minute as he fled through the doors and to the truck.

Keith wouldn't consider himself athletic, nor did he actively exercise as his doctor recommended, but the fact that he hadn't dropped Lyah the entire way was nothing short of a miracle.

He could feel the onslaught of a headache as he set a limp Lyah next to the truck. Craning his neck, he took note of no following footsteps.

They were in the clear.

Now, he had to figure out what to do. He had no experience hot wiring anything. Lyah's expertise would've been much appreciated at the moment. With shaky hands, he pushed open the driver's side door, not shocked that it was unlocked.

Did the owner lock anything?

Better luck for him, Keith thought. He slid Lyah into the truck as quickly as possible, careful not to hit her head, and placed her to lay down on the open middle seat. As he got in, he noticed the keys sitting on the dashboard.

Could this have been any easier? Keith looked above and shook his head with a smile. Someone was on his side today.

Though pressed for time, Keith took a moment to really think about what he was about to do or how everyone in his life would be disappointed in him if they ever found out what he was about to do. With one last breath, he looked at Lyah lying next to him, wounded and with no one to run to. She didn't have a home, any friends—nothing. And yet, she had it all.

Freedom.

Confidence.

Independence.

He envied her. Her ability to move so freely and not take life seriously. Her ability to laugh in the face of danger. He may have the things she didn't, but he wanted what she had.

No, he wasn't a risk-taker. But that didn't mean he couldn't start now. Keith turned the engine with one last glance at the barn and floored it off the property and into the unknown. And for once, he did it with a smile on his face.

Chapter Nine

Lyah

Lyah felt disoriented with a throbbing pain gushing throughout her body. Lyah's hand hovered over the bandaged area, feeling the tension intensify as she tried to get up and examine.

"Ow!" She blurted as she gave up trying to move. Laying in one spot for God knows how long had allowed the pain to settle in her muscles. She felt restricted.

"Hey! Hey! Be careful, you might start bleeding again." Keith took to her side by the bed with concern.

Wait, bed?

Lyah didn't remember getting out of the barn. How did they end up in a hotel room? Keith must've read the questions on her face because he started, "It's a long story. What matters is that we are safe for a while."

Lyah surveyed the room. It was cleaner than she was used to. The walls were white and inviting. The sofa in the studio complemented the space nicely in an ambiance. The bed was even fluffier. There was no way they were in a dingy motel.

Turning to Keith, Lyah asked, “Where are we?”

Keith hesitated but answered, “We’re on the outskirts of Wyoming.”

“Wyoming?! How long was I out?”

Lyah noted the splash of red in his eyes like he hadn’t slept in days. “About a day and a half. You had a fever and was in and out mostly. I treated you as best I could and kept driving.”

Had he stayed up the entire time?

Keith moved to the coffee maker by the makeshift kitchen and began to brew a fresh cup for her. “You should rest,” he said from across the room.

“No offense, but I think I’m fully rested. By the way, how did we afford this room?”

Keith didn’t answer until he brought her a cup and helped her ease into a sitting position to drink. “I used what I had to get a nice hotel room.”

Lyah looked at him in disbelief. “What about the rest of the way? Emergencies?”

“I have enough to get by, and frankly, so do you.”

“I’m not spending it if I can help it.”

“Why?” Keith asked.

“Because this is all I have until… I need it to last for a while.”

Lyah struggled to find the right words. She wasn't sure when she was going to get any more money or how. The thought of doing targets didn't seem to hold as much appeal since Target #32. Plus, there was Vegas to think about. Could she find something legitimate while she was there? Lyah couldn't tell Keith this, but she was tired of running. But what other choices did she have?

Lyah finished her cup, Keith silently taking it from her hands and putting it on the counter. She decided to voice her suspicion about the accident, "Do you think… do you think the accident was random? Because I don't."

Keith was quiet for a moment, his eyes distant. "Neither do I. The truck looked familiar." Lyah sat up straight. Keith continued, noting her troubled expression, "Do you remember when we went to the thrift store for the clothes? I've been trying to connect the dots that I'm not sure even exist, but there was this guy there that gave me the creeps."

"What guy?"

Keith rubbed his forehead. "When you were in the jewelry section staring at that ring, he was standing near you, staring with this creepy laser focus like he was going to do something." Lyah could tell he wanted to say more but he bit his tongue.

How had she not noticed the man in the store? The ring had taken all her focus. Her sixth sense didn't kick in. "What did he look like?"

Keith went on to describe the man. He sounded like someone from a mob but not anyone she knew. "He doesn't sound familiar, and I remember all my targets." Was it Target #32? He was obviously a drug handler or user or both. Maybe he had friends who could do favors like following them. Or men. She remembered him mentioning something like that. If that were the case, they were screwed.

Lyah tried not to think about what she'd gotten them into. As if reading her mind, Keith said, "If he's with the guy from the motel, I guess we'll find out eventually. If it is him, do you think he'll find us this far?"

"I don't know. If he does, I'll chalk it up to karma."

Keith scuffed, "Your karma, not mine."

Keith was right. Lyah quietly sat as she watched him fiddle through his duffel bag, pulling out an outfit. He briefly turned to her, struggling with a thought before shaking his head and heading to the bathroom.

As soon as the door closed, Lyah did her best to slide off the pearly white duvet without irritating the lingering pain in her leg. Considering she was in the same clothes since leaving the barn, she figured Keith hadn't touched her stash, so she bothered not to shuffle through her pockets. She struggled to make her way to the window, however.

There wasn't much of a view three stories up except for cars and traffic, but the gray skies and the slick road made it look rather cold. Lyah visibly shivered even though the room was nicely heated and backed away slowly from the window.

Lifting her shirt, she looked at the bandaged area. It stung to even bend slightly to look at it. There was red and purple discoloration that extended beyond the edges of the bandage. It looked terrible.

Had Keith really done all this himself? A feeling of appreciation filled her body. Guilt soon followed for how she had treated him before, especially in the barn. Even though what he said had hurt her, she knew she deserved it. For the things he was sacrificing to get them to Las Vegas and potentially putting his life in danger to keep them safe, she owed him a lot. A simple thank you could never suffice.

Lyah went to the counter to grab her mug. With as much haste as she could muster with her pain, she washed out the cup and used what was left of the half-pack of decaf coffee to make another cup.

By the time Keith was out of the shower and dressed in nighties, Lyah was waiting with a fresh cup of coffee as she sat on the twin bed she assumed was for Keith.

He paused and looked at her, then the cup, then back again with an eyebrow lifted. She eased off the bed and walked up to him, holding the cup out.

"Coffee?" Keith asked.

"For you."

"Me?"

Lyah nodded. "Just take it. I made it."

Keith looked unsure but slowly took the cup. He sniffed it, causing Lyah to roll her eyes.

"I didn't poison it. I promise."

"But why?" A sparkle of amusement passed his features.

He was going to make this difficult. With a sigh, Lyah said, "Just drink it. Do you question Starbucks when you buy coffee from them?"

"Well, no, considering I asked for it."

"You're insufferable!"

Keith could only chuckle as he took a gradual sip. A look of delight passed over his face, and Lyah felt satisfied knowing he liked it. Unsure what to do with herself, Lyah watched him place his old clothes in another bag and then pull out a fresh pair of gray sweatpants and a blue t-shirt with the words PRINCETON on it.

"Here," Keith said as he handed them to her.

Lyah knitted her eyebrows. "What are these for?"

"For your bath."

"But I have my own clothes. We went shopping, remember?"

Keith looked at the clothes in his hands and then frowned. "Right… Sorry, I must've forgotten."

Lyah eyed him carefully but took the clothes from him before he could take it away. His clothes were much more comfortable, she was sure. "I'll take them. I like wearing your clothes."

Clearing his throat, he replied, "Good. Great." Keith avoided her eyes and made his way to his bed and switched on the TV. Lyah took that as her cue of dismissal and grabbed what else she needed before heading to the bathroom and shutting the door.

Lyah could only stare at the bathroom upon walking inside. Though it wasn't anything notable to the average person, her perceptions of bathrooms over the last two years have been nothing to brag about.

The walls were covered in cream and caramel, giving it a honey hue that offered an inviting feeling. The floor tiles were also cream but clean enough to see the white seams. The shower was separate, providing a ceiling showerhead and glass panes. But what really caught her attention was the jet jacuzzi tub.

Naturally, she gravitated towards it and turned it on. As the tub began to fill, she found a bubble bath bottle and poured some in the jets. She giggled as a mountain of bubbles quickly formed, transporting her to the days of her youth when she enjoyed crashing into them. Taking off her clothes and carefully unwrapping her bandage, Lyah slipped into the warm waters and closed her eyes, wishing she could marinate in the pleasant feeling forever.

Though Lyah wanted to be free of thoughts, her mind ran to her past and present, questioning how she had gotten to this point in her life. She thought of her mom, cold and bitter, and likely living her best life without Lyah in it. She thought of her absentee father from her youth since he had traded in his family to a better imitation of a wife and daughter. She thought of James, a blimp in her life, but a story that never quite got the ending it deserved.

And then there was Keith—a stranger who, despite being in the clutches of danger, had stuck by her side to see the end of a journey. A stranger who disagreed with her choices and methods but tended to her wounds and entertained her terrible ideas.

Lyah thought of all the turmoil she's felt in the last few days—joy, fear, frustration, protection, guilt, and appreciation. It was the most she'd felt since running away two years ago. It was like her spirit awakened, and yet the idea of their journey coming to an end and having to face the reality of being alone again terrified her.

Keith had grown on her.

Would he remember her when the time came to part?

An unexpected tear slipped from her eye, and Lyah touched it as if it were foreign.

When was the last time she had cried?

A knock at the door had her scrambling to wipe her face. "Yes?" she called out.

"I'm ordering room service. Would you like anything?" Keith's muffled voice came through the door.

Lyah contemplated for a moment what she wanted to eat. "What do they have?"

"It's after five, so it's probably dinner time. Maybe roast chicken, steak, turkey, etc."

They all sounded good. Lyah simply couldn't choose. "I'll have what you're having."

There was a brief pause on his end before Keith answered, "Okay." She could hear him shuffle away from the door.

It would be another ten minutes before Lyah finally decided to exit the tub. Her hands had begun to prune, and she hated the feeling. Not to mention, the bubbles started to irritate her wound.

After letting out the water, Lyah stared at herself in the mirror for the first time in days. She noted her thin figure, not unnatural but less defined as usual. Heavy bags were situated under her eyes, and her wet hair was flat and stringy, unlike her regular bouncy brown curls. In short, she didn't recognize herself.

Not wanting to spend time picking at all her flaws, she swiftly brushed her teeth and dressed and wrapped her wound again before exiting the bathroom.

The aroma of roast chicken was the first thing that hit her nose. She followed the smell to the makeshift computer table by the window where Keith was unpacking the food. Surveying the table, she noted the array of choices.

Keith looked up at her as he tossed his last bag. "I didn't know what to get, so I got a little of almost everything. Figured we could save money on the road by taking the rest with us if we don't eat it all by then."

"Wow..." was all Lyah could manage to say. Her stomach somersaulted with hunger as she struggled to figure out what she wanted. Keith popped the liquor bottle she had forgotten about and poured them both a cup after handing her a paper plate.

Finally, after scarfing down what she could, they agreed to watch a movie they could find on the plasma TV as they lay on their respective beds. As Keith flipped through the channels, they happened upon The Titanic. Before he could change it, Lyah stopped him.

"Woah! Don't change it. This is perfect!"

"You mean corny," Keith mumbled but put the remote down.

"Corny? This is the best love story ever!" Lyah said with disbelief.

Keith turned to her with a frown. “Which part: the running or the drowning?”

Lyah could only gaze at him with her mouth agape. Never had she heard anyone slander The Titanic.

“You have no taste in movies.”

“I do, too. No one actually likes this movie. People are tickled by the story behind it and the Shakespearian ending. Otherwise, it’s a shit movie.”

“Okay, since you have such ‘special’ tastes, what’s your favorite movie?” Lyah asked with her arms crossed in defiance.

“Die Hard. That’s a classic.”

Lyah looked on in disgust. “Trash.”

“As is your choice,” Keith challenged.

“Agree to disagree?”

“Ditto.”

“But Titanic stays on.”

Keith rolled his eyes, assuming his earlier position but ultimately left the remote alone. “Okay, Rose.”

Lyah smiled and followed suit under covers and they enjoyed the rest of the movie in silence. Even with his earlier claims, Keith seemed engaged with the events until he slowly began to drift in and out of consciousness. Before sleep captured him, Lyah quietly called his name.

“Yeah?” Keith replied in a groggy tone.

“Why didn’t you leave me in the barn? I was practically dead weight."

"Did you want me to?"

No, she didn't. But she'd understand if he'd wanted to.

She didn't answer right away. "Thank you for sticking around."

When he didn't respond, she turned off her bedside lamp and snuggled under what she imagined to be heaven.

Chapter Ten

Keith

Because of Lyah's healing, Keith decided to stay another day in the hotel. It was unlikely that anyone would find them in the desolate town they were in if they were being followed, and at the very least, they could reenergize for the remainder of the trip. With the last night already upon them, and a few hours before dawn, Keith found himself unable to rest with the thoughts circling in his head.

Currently, Keith laid on his bed, face to the ceiling in the stark quiet while Lyah slept. Or so he thought.

"What are you thinking about?" Lyah asked as she shifted to face him. He took a quick peek at her before turning back to his blank space. Her hair was wild with curls, her eyes barely open and slightly covered by the white duvet like she was peeking out. It was adorable.

He shook the thought from his head. "Nothing. Everything. Both?"

With a grunt, Lyah pushed herself into a sitting position. "You know, when this is all over, you're going to look back and laugh. This is like a little bump in the road of an adventure you got to experience."

"Is that what this is to you? An adventure? Because it feels like a death race."

"Don't be ridiculous. The guy we stole from—"

"The guy that *you* stole from—"

"Whatever! The guy *I* stole from, he won't matter in the end. He won't follow us to Vegas. He won't ruin your chances with Tally if that's what you still want."

"If that's what I still want?"

Lyah shrugged. "If I'm honest, I'm beginning to think this trip is more for you than it is for Tally."

Keith let the words sink in. As the hours and days passed, his mind ran less and less on Tally. Understandably, they were technically on the run, but it was more than that. Keith wondered if the fear had somewhat turned into thrill and excitement for him.

True, this was the most excitement he ever experienced at the expense of possibly his life. He felt alive. He felt free. Would he always long for this feeling once it was gone?

And what of Tally? When he finally got a chance to see her, would he still want what he came for? Then, there was the issue of Tally reciprocating his offer. There was a high chance this could all go to shit. What would come of him then?

Those were the questions that plagued him more and more as

the nights wore on. And frankly, it scared him. His cross-country road trip with Lyah was becoming less about his mission and more about helping her.

Lyah.

Since the barn, things had become unexpectedly different between them. Less tension, more ease. Friendly and even comfortable. If Keith was honest with himself, he needed her on this journey with him as much as she needed him. Having her near him with her fearlessness and her street knowledge made him feel… invincible.

Well, no. He still shook in his boots at the thought of being caught or his parents finding out what he was up to.

But at the barn, the way he took charge, the way he felt driving off the lot with the owner's truck, the smile that was etched on his face as he barreled down the old beaten path—nothing could penetrate that feeling.

"I think you're right," Keith said.

It took her a moment to respond. He still hadn't removed his eyes from the ceiling, so he assumed she repositioned judging by the scuffle he heard.

"I'm sorry, my ears must be busted. What did you say?"

Keith chuckled. "I said you're right."

"About?"

"About everything. About me and this 'adventure' we're on. It gives me a feeling…"

"What kind of feeling?" Lyah pressed.

"I don't know," Keith began. "Thrill, maybe? The thrill of fear? I can't say it without sounding like an idiot."

Lyah sighed. "You're not an idiot, Keith. You just know what it feels like to be in my shoes."

Keith laid quiet as Lyah got up from her bed and sat on the edge of his. With confusion marred on his face, he scrutinized her position next to him. "What are you doing?"

Lyah smiled as she matched his position on the bed, face up. "I'm bonding with you. Congratulations, you're the first person I've ever admitted that to."

"Bond with you?"

"Yeah," Lyah said, barely above a whisper.

With her so close to him, his skin felt tingly. It was strange. "Have you ever had friends?"

Lyah shook her head. "Not for the lack of effort, though. Usually, if someone wanted to be my friend, it was because they needed something from me. I've always been… used."

The irony of their situation wasn't lost on him. A gnawing feeling filled his stomach, hearing those words. Was it pity? Did he fall into that category after what he revealed to her?

"So, you've never been close to anyone? I find that hard to believe if I'm honest." For a girl with such spunk, she seemed like someone to always have people falling for her charms.

Had he fallen for it, too?

It was Lyah's turn to fall silent in thought. When she spoke up, her voice had taken on a melancholy tone. “There was someone. James. Probably the only person I can think of that ever really cared for me.”

“James? So, you did have a boyfriend?”

Lyah craned her neck to the side to look at him. “No. We were never friends, nor were we ‘together,’ but we agreed to use each other when needed. We had an understanding.”

“But?”

“I ran. I ran because I couldn’t give him what he deserved. We had an understanding, but I always sensed he wanted something more from it. I’m not capable of providing that kind of feeling.”

“How do you know you’re not just telling yourself you can’t? Are you afraid to love?”

“I don’t know.”

Keith suspected she was despite her answer. It would explain her choice of living, always on the run, never being tied down to anyone or anything. Frankly, it was hard picturing Lyah as a girl in love. A doting girlfriend. A girl with ambitions. It sounded ignorant, but the girl before him was never vulnerable. Knowing her story, it was everything he suspected, but at the same time, he wished she got a chance to experience those feelings. Maybe she thought she didn’t deserve love or that no one cared for her.

What kind of life was that to live?

Keith held a whole new perspective of her. He felt selfish for having experienced the things that Lyah never had and complaining about it. His whole life had been planned and projected for him. He’d been in love, and he had dreams.

What did Lyah have?

Turning to her, Keith began, "I know we've knocked heads in the past—well, recently—but you're not so bad. Stubborn and shaky, but not bad."

Lyah laughed. "I think that's the nicest thing you've ever said to me."

Keith smiled. "Yeah, it is."

"You're not so bad, either. A pain in my ass and a bit uptight, but not bad."

Keith burst out in a full-hearted laugh. "You know, even though our lives are practically in danger and I'm probably in a boatload of trouble with my folks, not to mention the police at this point, I don't think I could ever remember a time I felt so…"

"Free?"

Keith nodded. "Yeah. Free. Is this what you feel all the time? Is this why you don't want to go back home?"

Lyah chewed on her lower lip. "No."

Keith frowned. "No?"

"I don't feel free. I haven't felt free until you picked me up at the gas station. I ran away from home because there was nothing left for me there. There was *no one* left for me there. I've never had support. I was always free in retrospect, but I was always bound by negativity in my life, from the people around me. So, I ran from it. But it follows me wherever I go. With every decision I make. With every person I meet. It's there like chains pulling me away from the good things that I can have."

His heart felt solemn hearing those words. "I'm sorry."

Lyah shook her head with a looming smile. "My apologies were left back home."

Keith yawned and stretched. "I hope we can get to Vegas in one piece."

"I don't doubt it. We're a team."

Keith quirked his eyebrows. "We're a team now? We went from mere enemies to a team in a matter of days. I call that a win."

"I call that a 180 and head spin."

"Does this mean no more fighting?"

Lyah turned to him with a side-eye. "I don't know. Does it? You're the one that always starts it."

"I do not!"

"Yes, you do! All the time. You always have something mean-spirited to say or find some way to degrade me."

It was true most of the time. If he'd took the time to understand her before, he would've understood why she acted the way she did. He felt the infliction of pain in her voice. The gnawing in his stomach grew. "I'm really sorry, Lyah. I truly am."

Lyah turned away. "It's okay. I'm sure I need work, too." That was her way of apologizing, he understood.

"You're headstrong and stubborn. But that just means you know what you want and don't settle," Keith admitted.

"And you're an angry control freak, but that's likely because you've had your whole life planned for you and are stressed."

"Right on the money."

"Ditto."

Keith picked at the lint on his clothes. "Where are you going to go when we separate in Vegas? What are you going to do?"

"There's always something to do in Vegas. So many places to see."

"That's vague."

"It's also true," Lyah countered.

She was avoiding the question, perhaps because she really didn't know. Hell, he wasn't even sure what *he* would do once he got to Vegas. Would he drop her off at a bus station or a hotel? On the side of the road, maybe? The thought of that felt wrong.

Maybe she could be useful in Vegas for his own mission. Though she had offered before, he'd never taken her seriously. His plan was always to separate as soon as they reached Vegas. But would this new plan constitute him using her? Maybe if he asked, it wouldn't. The thought lifted the guilt from his chest.

Without thinking, he found himself asking, "Why don't you help me with Tally?"

Lyah sat up, her eyes widened. "Really?" Perhaps she had forgotten her offer.

Keith shrugged, suddenly embarrassed to ask. "Yeah. I'm going to need help getting there and trying to talk to her. You might be able to help me prep or distract her fiancé."

Lyah tried to suppress a smile, but it broke through anyway.

Keith frowned. "What?"

"Are you getting soft on me?"

Heat rose to his face. "N-No, I—"

Suddenly, a weight was over his upper body. It took him a moment to realize it was Lyah trying to hug him. With her hair in his face, he could smell the hotel shampoo's flowery scent.

"Thank you," Lyah breathed in his ear.

She pulled off him before he could even react. Keith cleared his throat and sat up, matching her resumed position as he thought about what he had just gotten himself into.

A brief pause descended upon them. Lyah looked at her bed then back at him. "I should get back to my bed."

She didn't wait for an answer. Instead, she made her way to her original spot on her bed and covered herself with the duvet. He waited until she got comfortable before speaking. "You're wrong, you know."

With her voice muffled by the sheet, she answered, "About?"

"You do have a friend." If it wasn't for the fact that he was about to doze off, he would've seen the smile on Lyah's face that she didn't try to hide.

Chapter Eleven

Lyah

"I'm not letting you drive, Lyah!"

"But I'm feeling much better!"

"It doesn't mean you should be driving. Besides, we have to keep a low profile, and you can't drive all that well."

"That crash wasn't my fault," Lyah huffed as she crossed her arms. Keith ignored her as he placed his duffel bag in the bed of the truck.

Lyah had been arguing with Keith for the last hour about letting her drive. His excuse was her wound, but it felt a whole lot better since getting injured. All the sleep she was able to get helped plenty, even for her leg. Truthfully, she felt terrible that he had driven all the way to the hotel and wanted to pay him back by driving the rest of the way, but he wasn't having it.

So much for not fighting.

Feeling the weight of her silence, Keith approached her gently, his edge from earlier gone. "Look, we need to get out of here soon, and I can't risk you getting hurt again. It'll slow us down. We have maybe a day left of driving if we don't take any more hotel stops or find ourselves in more trouble. So, can we not fight about this? Please?"

A day? In a day, it could all be over. The thought left a bitter taste in her mouth. Nodding, Lyah took his lead into the truck.

The beginning of the ride was plagued with thoughts of what they'd gone through since meeting almost a week ago. In that short amount of time, Keith had grown on her. Dare she say she trusted him, even? It was the wildest and scariest and most fulfilling moments of her life compacted into a few days with a stranger.

Just a few hours before, they laid in bed, bonding on levels she thought she would never. She could never say this to Keith's face, but she felt safe with him. She felt like she had a real friend.

A few days ago, she would've never thought she'd say that about Keith. The aggravating, know-it-all, control freak who argued about any and everything concerning her had become someone she could confide in. It was a head twister.

And though they hadn't talked about it since he mentioned it, Lyah embraced the excitement of being a part of Keith's plan to win back Tally, whatever it was. The excitement was mixed with more curiosity, however. Though she had some idea about Tally, Keith never delved into their backstory or why he thought this whole trip was a good idea. It was like he was blindly going off expectations. But

Lyah kept those thoughts to herself for fear he might change his mind.

She didn't want to be alone again. She also couldn't go back to her old habits. How could she ever go back to her old lifestyle after getting a taste of a real connection? She never felt that anywhere, not even at home.

Home. Lyah thought about her mother. Did her mother miss her at all? Would her mother ever welcome her back with open arms should the time come, or would she be treated like the ghost she'd become? Was she looking for Lyah?

Since leaving home, Lyah had no contact with her mother. She had no idea if she had called the authorities in search of her or even if her father knew that she disappeared in the wind.

Did anyone care that she was gone?

Lyah spent every opportunity away from watching the news or using anything to link her to her home life, believing it was for the best. But there were times like now that she wondered.

The questions continued to swirl until Lyah's mood deflated further as they traveled along the country roads.

"Are you okay?" Keith asked, glanced at her briefly.

Lyah shook out of her stupor. "Yeah, I'm fine. Just thinking."

"About?"

"Everything and anything," Lyah said with a weak smile. To sway him, she threw out, "Do you know where in Vegas Tally is staying?"

Keith took a moment to answer. "I have an idea. There's this hotel she raved about back then that she wanted to visit on a road trip.

They have one in Vegas."

"When is the wedding supposed to be?"

"Saturday, I think."

Lyah frowned. "You think?"

"The days are running into each other. To be honest, I'm not even sure I know what day today is."

"It's Thursday…"

Keith groaned. "Already?"

Lyah winced. "You seriously didn't know it was Thursday? We had a calendar in the hotel room."

Keith grabbed his hair. "I didn't think to check. I thought it was Tuesday or something."

"Yikes," Lyah mumbled. "We still have time. If she's at the hotel where you think she is, maybe this can be a quick thing."

"What's quick about it? I would need to convince her she's making a big mistake and call off her wedding within a day, maybe a few hours."

Lyah nibbled her lip in concentration. She didn't want to ask for fear of his answer but pushed the envelope anyway. "Are you going to convince her to leave with you?"

Keith seemed stumped by the question. Had he not thought that far? Lyah wanted to slap her forehead.

"Ugh…"

"I'm going to take that as an 'I have no real plan.'"

Keith threw her a glare. "I do have a plan, it's just more of an outline."

"An outline doesn't give you supporting details, much like your plan. Keith, if I'm going to help you win this girl, I need details."

"Fine! I may ask her to come with me, but she may not come with me anyway."

"Why not?"

"Tally hasn't seen me in months, and for me to just show up and try to take her away would be…" Keith paused as if he was digesting his words for the first time.

"Be what, Keith?"

He didn't answer. Instead, his mouth was agape, a frown etched on his face as he stared off at the end of the road.

"Keith?" Lyah tried again.

"Stupid. This is all stupid. Why am I doing this? Why did I think this was ever going to work?" Keith started talking to himself.

"Keith?" Lyah said with worry.

"She's never going to leave with me. She doesn't want to see me. She's made that clear the last time we saw each other. I'm wasting my time."

"Keith!"

Keith jumped. He turned to Lyah with slight panic. "What am I doing, Lyah?"

Time to put on her big girl panties.

"You're fighting for what you want. That's what you're doing."

"What if it's not? What if this whole thing was for nothing?"

"Then at least you know you tried. You said it yourself, you've always had your life planned for you. Handed to you. You did this on your own. You took your own initiative, and you went out and tried to get what you wanted. And if it doesn't work out in your favor, so what? At least you know you tried. That's more than a lot of people can say."

Keith tightened and loosened his grip on the steering wheel. "What if it's not what I want anymore? What if you were right—that this whole trip was about the adventure and getting away and not about Tally?"

Lyah didn't know what to say to that. He was having second thoughts, which was expected, but it sounded like he was coming to his senses. Though the gesture sounded like a girls' dream on paper, the fact that he was driving thousands of miles across the country to stop the wedding of a girl who no longer wanted him was a bad idea. Even worse, he had no plan, no idea what he wanted out of it, and no backup.

Was she supposed to tell him that he was making all the wrong choices?

A true friend would. But he needed to learn for himself as well. Telling him wasn't her call, and she knew that. Keith would have to find out on his own. Only then would he realize that he wasn't running to Tally; he was running away from home, too.

Lyah put on a brave face. "Then, I guess we'll find out, won't we?"

Keith's face was marred with confusion. "What do you mean?"

"I mean, we need to see this through. *You* need to see this through. Not just for Tally, but for your own peace of mind."

Keith nodded slowly. "You're right."

"I'm always right," Lyah snuck in.

"Don't ruin the moment, Lyah."

"Too late!" Lyah reached over to the radio and switched the channel to an oldie's station currently playing Tina Turner's *What's Love*?

Lyah started to belt out the words of the song, Keith giving her the wildest look ever. But she didn't care. It was likely going to be one of the last days she would spend in his presence. The least she could do was make it memorable, not for him, but for her.

Keith turned the music down once the song was over a few minutes later. "I never pegged you for a Tina Turner fan."

"Yeah, neither did I."

"I'll add that to the mental list of things I didn't know."

Lyah quirked an eyebrow at him. "There's a list?"

"Well, yeah. Don't you have one?"

Lyah shook her head. "I didn't, but I will now. What's on your list? Maybe I'll provide some answers."

Keith squared his shoulders as if preparing for battle. "I have more questions than answers, so I'll start there. For starters, why did you steal the money?"

"I needed cash, and I thought he was an easy grab."

Keith snorted. "But why not give it back once he found out about it? You could've mended the situation and found another target."

It was Lyah's turn to snort. "This isn't the movies. He would've hurt me one way or the other. Especially since he thought I was a street girl."

"But you are, aren't you?"

"By name, not by action. I never had sex with the men I stole from," Lyah scowled.

Keith saw the less than pleasant look on her face. "I'm sorry, I didn't mean to insinuate you being a hooker. I meant you know more about the streets than the average person."

Lyah waved him off, her defensiveness dissolving. "It's whatever. Regardless, I would've likely gotten shot or hurt in some other way if he caught me sooner, taking the money."

"So that's your… system of survival?"

His question wasn't mean-spirited or assuming, but it did irritate her not because he asked—rather, she felt like the worse person facing what she'd done in the past.

Lyah nodded.

"Yes, that's my system."

"Why not just get a job or freelance or something? Doesn't that get tiring?"

Lyah had thought about it, even attempted it once. Getting a job wasn't the hard part. Holding one was the issue. She was offered the position to bartend non-alcoholic drinks in a bar she was frequenting, and it was great for a month, but she itched to leave. Stability wasn't her thing. Eventually, she went and found her "calling."

"I've tried it, but it's not my thing. I'm not actually good at anything besides what I'm doing now."

Keith frowned. "That's not true."

"You barely know me. How would you know?"

"Because everyone has something they're good at."

"Is that what they tell you at Princeton University?"

Keith swung wild eyes are her. Almost accusatory. "How did you know I attend Princeton?" Did he not realize he paraded Princeton on his clothes?

Lyah rolled her eyes at his accusatory eyes. "I didn't go through your wallet. You had a sweater on the night we met and sometime after that. It had your school name on it."

"Oh."

"Yeah, 'Oh.'"

"I didn't mean to—"

"It's not a big deal, Keith. Just drop it, please."

So much for trust.

As they drove, silence permeated the air, stifling them both. Just when they were getting somewhere, he had to ruin it. Did he really think she had gone through his things? If she wanted to rob him, she would've done it the night they met. Granted, she was guilty of thinking about it, but she didn't see the need to. The cash she had on hand would last a good while on her own.

"Lyah? I'm sorry. I wasn't trying to accuse you, I swear."

She knew she was assuming. Granted, he hadn't said anything to note accusation from his end. Perhaps this was her way of trying to push him away before their fateful departure. Lyah peered out of the window at the desert land and mountains of Wyoming. There was barely anyone on the long stretch of road. There wasn't a store or gas station in sight. Lyah found herself wondering if they had enough gas to carry them that far.

In another life, she'd like to live out west where the areas were quiet, and the streets were small and less busy. Much different from the bustling city she grew up in. It must be nice to get peace in a town that barely speaks. When she ran out of options, she might find herself out west with a herd.

She wondered if she would like Las Vegas. Reading about it and hearing people talk about it in the past made her curious enough to wonder about life there. And if she didn't like it, maybe she'd find herself on the Cali beaches.

Has Keith ever been anywhere besides where he lived?

Lyah looked over at him and looked away then back at him again. He must've felt her eyes because he asked, "What? Why are you looking at me?"

"Have you been west before?"

Keith shook his head. "Before now, I've never been anywhere but Florida to see my grandparents. Why?"

Lyah shrugged. "Just wondering. It seems so peaceful on this side of the country."

"And horror movie-ish. If we broke down out here, we'd likely be murdered by the next morning."

Lyah gave him a deadpan look. "Way to be morbid. It's probably no more dangerous than the eastside."

"I beg to differ. There are easier ways to dispose of a body out here, considering no one is here."

Lyah tapped her chin in thought. "You have a point."

"Are you thinking about staying on this side of the country?"

"I don't know. I'll see what Vegas has to offer, and then I'll decide."

"Well, whatever you decide, find somewhere that offers everything you're looking for."

"As in...?"

"I don't know. Tell me."

Lyah paused. What was she looking for?

"I can't say."

Keith blinked. "You can't say or won't say?"

"It means I don't know. I don't know what I'm looking for."

"What makes you happy? Your freedom? Your ability to utilize your street-smart? Meeting new people?"

"Are you interviewing me?"

Keith laughed. "No! Believe it or not, I'm trying to help you. When we go our separate ways, are you going back to what you did before, or are you going to try and live a normal life?"

It was such a deep question that Lyah shifted several times in her seat. Did she want to live a normal life? Could she? Was there such a thing as normal in her life?

She couldn't fully answer that. It was one thing to fantasize about living "normal," but would that life ever be fulfilling to her? Or would she find ways to sabotage it and end up back on the streets?

Lyah couldn't trust herself to stay true to that life. She barely had an education; she had no support. What would come of it?

But instead of voicing those concerns, Lyah took on a brave face and responded, "I'll take whatever life gives me."

Chapter Twelve

Lyah

Las Vegas.

It seemed like forever ago they had set out on this journey. After a grueling twenty-hour drive, they had finally reached their destination: The FlyBy Hotel and Spa.

It was bittersweet, though. The idea of getting a glimpse into Keith's life was exciting but knowing this was the end of her stop made her stomach drop. Lyah hated goodbyes. Would she know when it was time to let go?

Lyah shook the thoughts from her head. After all, she had spent practically the entire ride thinking about it.

As they turned into the hotel parking lot, dread overcame her. Spying a glance at Keith, it looked as if he also was coming to terms with their destination, whether out of dread or nervousness, she wasn't sure.

"We're here," he said matter of fact.

Lyah struggled to open her mouth, unsure of how to respond. Thankfully, he decided to continue.

"We should brainstorm."

"Brainstorm?" she asked.

"Yeah. I can't just walk in there. What if she's with him? We have to get them out of their room and apart."

"Do you even know what this guy looks like? Or his name?"

"I think his name is Jim. No, Jason. Or was it James? Can you imagine if it was your James? That would've been awkward…" Keith trailed off.

Lyah stilled for a moment, a flash of a familiar face rolling through her eyes. The name was popular. There was no reason to think it could be her the James of her past. "It's funny you partly remember his name. Have you been stalking him?"

Keith frowned, but she could see his eyes flitting. He has stalked the poor guy. "It's not like I was going to do anything to him. I only searched his socials a few times to know who my competition was. All I cared about was Tally."

Cared?

Lyah wondered if he knew what he said. A part of her wondered why he was still going through with this. Even with her encouragement the day before and the meaning behind the trip, she half expected him to call the whole thing off. Did he feel like he would've wasted his time turning back now? It was clear Tally was a second thought.

Either way, she had promised to help, and she wasn't backing down from it. With a deep sigh, Lyah said. "Fine. I'll somehow get them distracted. But we still need to find out what room they're in and how to get past the lobby. This isn't like back in the days when you can just walk on in."

Keith thought for a moment. "We could pretend we're part of the family for the wedding. I heard she's having a private ceremony in the hotel. We could pretend to be a surprise."

"That's not going to work. Maybe pretend we forgot our key card and give Tally's name? Wait, no, they'd be suspicious without ID. Do you think Tally would get the honeymoon suite?"

Keith snapped his fingers. "That's it. We can go to the desk, ask for a honeymoon suite, and guide the questions until they hint at where their biggest rooms are."

"But how do we even know Tally and her groom are going to be in those rooms?"

"Trust me, I know Tally."

Lyah scrunched her nose. "But she's getting married in Vegas. That literally spells cheap and quick."

Keith threw her a frown. "I know Tally."

He started to get out of the car, Lyah following close behind. "Keith, what if this doesn't work? What if we're not convincing enough, and we can't find them in time? What then?"

Keith stopped short; his eyebrows lifted in curiosity. "Are you having second thoughts, Lyah?"

"What? No, I just don't think we've thought this through enough."

"Is that really it? Because I've never known you to back down on your word. I'm not forcing you to help me, but you're the only one who can. If there's anyone who can get this done, it's you. You have charisma. You can talk anyone into anything."

Lyah started to object but decided against it. He was right. But was that to be taken as a compliment?

Lyah sighed. "Okay, let's do this. I'll put on my best act."

Keith grabbed her by the shoulders in an unexpected hug. "Thank you!" he breathed out. Lyah, being squished against his chest, tried to respond, but his shirt's fabric was in her way. He let her loose not too long after and cleared his throat as if embarrassed by what he's just done.

"I think we should head in."

"I agree," Lyah said, trying to stifle a laugh as she walked past him into the lobby.

The hotel wasn't anything fancy or breathtaking, but it was a lot better than the ones Lyah stayed in recent years, sans the last one in Wyoming. It set off a sense of serenity in the bustling shuffle around them.

There was a short line in front of them. By the time they made it to the front desk, Lyah had already grabbed Keith's arm as if they were smitten.

"Do you have to grab me so hard?" Keith whispered as the couple in front of them started toward the elevators.

"Do you want to do this or not? Quit complaining," Lyah shot back.

The woman at the desk, whose nametag read Mary, ushered them forward. "Welcome to The FlyBy Hotel & Spa! How can I help you today?"

Lyah was the first to speak. "Hi Mary, we need your finest room available. I and my husband-to-be need a honeymoon suite so we can get well acquainted if you know what I mean." Lyah threw in a wink to prove her point.

She could feel Keith's embarrassment radiating off him if his warm skin was any indication. Mary blushed and looked at her computer, typing something in. "We don't usually have our honeymoon suite available same-day, but I'll take a look… Sorry, we only have one deluxe room available."

Lyah pretended to be bummed. "Oh, baby, I told you they wouldn't have a room available."

Keith looked uneasy but nonetheless tried to appear as if he was sad about it. Mary asked. "Would you like to book the deluxe room instead?"

Lyah placed a finger on her chin. "I don't know. Babe, what do you think?"

Keith's eyes widened, obviously not expecting to speak during the entire exchange. "Um… I-I think we should go somewhere else?"

"Looks like we'll have to go elsewhere. For future reference, Mary, if we wanted to come back in the future, what can we expect with the honeymoon suites?"

"Well, both honeymoon suites have a jacuzzi in the room, a king-sized bed, balcony with an amazing view from the top floor over the city and comes with complimentary room services and spa discounts."

Checkmate. "Thank you so much, Mary. Come, babe, let's go check out the other hotels."

Keith looked ready to object, but Lyah hoped he trusted what she was about to do. She feigned like they were walking away but stopped abruptly and turned back to Mary with a snap of her finger.

"You know, Mary. We may be on the road for a while. Would you happen to have a restroom nearby? I don't want to ride around with a full bladder."

Mary nodded unsuspectingly. "Sure! If you take the hall to the right and make a sharp left, the restrooms are right ahead."

Lyah smiled. "Thank you so much, Mary! Honey, you don't mind waiting in the car for me, would you?"

Keith stared at her for a moment but finally got what she was saying and nodded before walking off. Lyah high-tailed it to the ladies' restroom, making sure to look around for an elevator. Sure enough, there was an elevator right before the restrooms. A back door was off to the side of it. It was like God had aligned all the answers for her.

Lyah entered the bathroom for only a moment for appearances and then walked to the back door. Carefully, she opened it and was surprised to see Keith waiting right next to it.

"Huh. I thought I'd have to wait the whole day for you," Lyah said as she let him in.

Keith scoffed. "I think we should've just rented the deluxe room and call it a day. It would've been easier. And why not just let me go to the bathroom with you?"

"Because in case I got caught, you'd still be able to get away. Plus, Mary needed to know we didn't plan to stick around. And getting the room wouldn't have been smart. We'd have to wait for them to clean it and lose out on money that we may need. Besides, this is thrilling. Now come. There's an elevator over here."

Lyah surveyed the area as she led him to the elevator. "What's the plan from here? We can't knock on all the doors."

"We could pull all the fire alarms," Lyah joked.

Keith snorted. "Sounds like a felony charge and a loss of future—namely mine."

Lyah laughed. "I was kidding. I'll think of something when we get to the top floor. Maybe we might get lucky."

The elevator dinged, and they stepped in, Lyah pressing the button for the eighth floor. When the elevator doors closed, Keith turned to her.

"So… this is our last day together granted all goes well," Keith stated.

With her eyes glued to the floor number changing, Lyah responded. "That it is."

"Do you plan to stay here at the hotel, or should I drive you somewhere? I don't know how we're supposed to part."

Lyah stayed silent, trying to hold back the stinging in her eyes. She didn't know either but right now was not the time she wanted to talk about it. "Keith, we'll cross that bridge when we get there."

Thankfully, he didn't push back. When the elevator doors opened, Lyah led the way out. "Mary implied there were two rooms, so we need to find out which ones are the honeymoon suites. Usually, they have a bigger entranceway, but no two hotels are the same."

"Or we could ask the housekeeper," Keith said, pointing to the housekeeper pulling out towels from her cart in front of an open room.

"Good point." Grabbing his arm again, they made their way to the petite lady in her gray and white uniform.

"Excuse me, could you tell us where to find the honeymoon suites? My fiancé and I just checked in, but we forgot the directions," Lyah said.

The old lady looked confused at first, and Lyah hoped she didn't realize the honeymoon suites hadn't been cleaned for new vacationers since they were already occupied. Thankfully, the lady nodded and pointed to the end of the hall.

"Across the hall from each other, the last doors." The lady turned back to her task, leaving no room for a response. Lyah still thanked her as they both headed down the hall.

"Do we have a plan yet?" Keith anxiously asked. "We're getting closer to our destination, and still, I have no idea what we are doing."

Lyah stopped him in the middle of the hall, her hands restraining his arms. "Keith, I know you're nervous. I can practically feel you shaking in my arms but follow my lead. Before we get to the doors, I want you to hide. I'll knock on both doors, lead out the groom and when you see me pass by, you go in and do your thing. You got that?"

Keith nodded slowly. "And then what? How long do I have?"

Lyah shrugged. "I'll try for 20 mins, if not longer. If I'm not back by then, find a way to get her out of the room in case he gets back. In fact, do that first. I'll take him to the first floor outside. Maybe say something is wrong with the wedding stuff. You have free reign everywhere else."

"Where do we meet up after?"

Lyah wasn't sure if she would see him after this. Her plan, though not well thought out, was to leave without telling him. Lyah took a good look at him and said the only thing she could. "In the truck. We'll meet in the truck."

He seemed satisfied with that answer. With a bob of his head, he responded, "Okay. Sounds doable. I can't believe I'm about to do this."

Lyah gave him a genuine smile. With a gentle tap on his cheek with her hand, she said, "You'll be just fine. Just tell her what your heart is feeling. I'm sure she'll appreciate it at the very least."

"Thanks, Lyah. Thank you for this."

"Don't mention it. Now, let's get this over with."

They continued their way to the end of the hall, Keith taking Lyah's word and hiding near a sitting area with a view. Before knocking on the first door, Keith gave her a thumbs up, which she smiled at. Taking a deep breath, Lyah hesitantly knocked on the door. The door opened to a middle-aged red-headed woman who looked rather annoyed to be answering the door.

"Can I help you?" she asked in a dismissive tone.

For once, Lyah struggled to find the right words. This couldn't be the right room. "Hi. I'm looking for someone named Tally? I have some information on her wedding that needs urgent attention."

The lady pressed her lips together, sizing Lyah up. "There is no one here named Tally. Now, if you'll excuse me, I have some business to finish."

The door slammed in Lyah's face, and she was tempted to flick off the old shrewd. Turning around, Lyah decided to try her luck at the last door. She prayed Tally was behind this one.

With a light knock, Lyah waited patiently for someone to come to the door. She heard a male voice say, "Coming!" when she decided to knock again after a few moments.

All the emotions she was feeling sucked right out of her body when the door finally opened. She was prepared for everything but this. Standing before her with a matching look of shock and a shirt half hanging around his neck and over one arm, was James.

Her James.

She couldn't speak, nor could she move. She was delighted to see him and see that he was well, but in Vegas… that was not something she expected. Many questions filled her brain, and Lyah made a strangling sound as she opened her mouth, but James beat her to it.

"Lyah? W-What are you doing here? How did you find me?"

Did he think she came to see him? Maybe that could be her angle, she thought. But she needed to know if he was getting married but now for an entirely different reason. "Uh, I was in the hotel and heard about a wedding, and then your name popped up. Thought I'd come to say congratulations. Maybe even talk? I hope this isn't a bad time…" She hoped he wouldn't ask how she found the room.

James frowned. "I didn't know the wedding was that popular with the staff. It's a small gathering. In fact, our family isn't going to be here."

"I guess the hotel staff is just excited, then," Lyah lied.

James looked behind him and stepped out, closing the door behind him. He pulled his shirt on properly, and thankfully as Lyah was getting flashbacks of doing things she long forgot about.

"I don't even know what to say. I can't believe you're here. I have so many questions," James said.

"Maybe we should talk somewhere else. I have some time to spare. We could walk outside and catch up."

James nodded. "Yeah, let's do that. Let me tell Tally I'll be gone for a bit." He went back into the room and closed it behind him.

"*Psst!*" Lyah called out to Keith. He looked around the corner with hopeful eyes, and Lyah gave him a thumbs up. He whispered a "*Yes!*" and hid in his spot again. James came back out right then with fresh sneakers and a smile.

"Let's go, shall we?"

As they walked past where Keith was hiding, Lyah gave him one last glance and a weak smile. He mouthed, "*Thank you,*" and left to his destination. When they reached the elevators, Lyah took a shaky breath and watched the doors shut as if the last chapter in her life had closed.

Chapter Thirteen

Lyah

"How've you been? I've always wondered what happened to you after we parted. You never returned my calls," James said once they reached outside. Lyah had geared him towards the back of the building to a pathway through a garden for a stroll.

Such a loaded question. Where did she even begin? Could she tell him the truth? In the past, he knew almost everything about her life, mostly the bad. But it's been two years since they saw each other. Things change, people change, and he was getting married. His life was good. Why bother him with the negative parts of her life anymore?

So, Lyah decided to stretch the truth instead. "I've been good. Living on my own, taking a cross-country road trip."

James smiled. "That's good to hear. I'm glad you've been well after everything back home..."

Lyah waved him off. If only he knew. "I wasn't going to let her control my life. My mother needed a beating stick, and I refused to let it be me."

"So, you're in a good place now?" He asked it as if he was testing her. Lyah thought about the last week with Keith and her adventures. Though they weren't entirely out of the woods, she felt better in the last week than she had in the past two years, if not, ever.

Lyah nodded. "Yeah, I'm in a good place. What about you? Being married is something I didn't know you wanted. Hell, I didn't know you'd do it in Vegas."

James chuckled and stuffed his hands into his pockets. "I didn't think I'd get married either. But Tally, she's different. We hit it off as soon as we met, and I felt like I would've been wasting time if I didn't propose."

A sense of longing overtook Lyah for something she never was able to feel. Love. She could tell James was in love. It was bittersweet knowing she would never feel that way or have someone feel that way about her. But she felt joy in knowing he was happy. James was the closest thing she'd ever had to friend back then. It was nice to know he went down the right path, unlike her.

"How did the two of you meet?" She was curious. After all, Keith was limiting in his details about Tally, especially in the beginning.

"We met on campus during class one day. Turns out, we were studying the same minor. We talked, found out we had a lot in common, and went for drinks. By the next month, we were official and now, here."

"Sounds like love at first sight." He was silent to that which drew her attention. "No…?"

James bit his lower lip and stopped walking, Lyah following suit. He smiled tentatively and said, "No. It was love at first date. There's only been one person who I fell in love with at first sight."

Lyah was trying to read his eyes, but her own widened when she realized what he was saying. She shook her head adamantly. "No, there's no way."

"Yes, way."

"No."

James laughed. "Yes. Lyah, believe it or not, you're mesmerizing in the most annoying way possible."

Lyah rolled her eyes as she continued walking. "Is that supposed to be a compliment?"

"I'm saying you're hard to get through, so I knew I never stood a chance because you never felt that way about me and probably never would. I respected your wishes to stay the way we were, using each other. But I did love you. I still do."

Lyah felt like the wind got knocked out of her and barely caught herself from falling. No one had ever said that to her before. James? He was a great person, and he helped her through some tough times in the past, but love was something she was blind to. She thought he was as well.

"I don't know what to say," Lyah said. "I didn't know."

"I didn't expect you to. I wasn't planning on telling you. Ever. But now that you're here, I think it's important for you to know."

"Why?"

"Because you still have that look in your eyes. The lost look. The sad look. What aren't you telling me?" It was like he could see right through her. She started to panic and had a quick fight or flight moment.

"It's nothing, James. You don't need to be worrying about me. I can handle myself. I have for this long, and I'm doing fine. You're getting married, and I'm so happy for you, and I hope you get everything you want."

Lyah was choosing flight even though she wanted to stay back and talk, but James wasn't done with her. "Please don't run, Lyah. Aren't you tired of running?"

She turned around with her eyes blazing. "I don't run. I walk away."

"Walk. Run. Lyah, you deserve all the things you want for me," James said as he grabbed her shoulder. "Why won't you allow yourself to be happy?"

"Who says I'm not? Maybe I am happy where I am in life."

"Lyah, your mouth says that, but your eyes don't tell lies. I may not know everything about you because you never fully let me in, but I always knew that look. You're running from something. Is that why you found me today?"

Even though the truth was at the tip of her tongue, she didn't say it. It wasn't her secret to tell, and she wanted to protect what little time Keith had with Tally. "It was pure coincidence we ended up in the hotel. But I needed my closure." Lyah wasn't sure if that was true or not.

Being on the road with Keith had opened her eyes to some things but seeing James made her want to officially close that chapter of her life. Her past. Lyah was ready to get on with her future. Maybe seeing James was less of a coincidence and more of a sign.

"I don't think it was," James said. "I think you coming a day before my wedding is a sign that maybe I needed to close this part of my life. And maybe you do, too. But I think it reminded me that you've taught me a lot in the time we spent together. Even though you never felt the same, I'm grateful you let me experience it with you."

Lyah usually didn't like deep conversations, but she needed to hear that. It felt like a weight had flown off her shoulder. "Thank you for being patient with me. For trying. That's more than anyone has ever done for me."

"Thank you for allowing me as much as you could."

They walked further on the path, passing a few people enjoying what was left of the hour. It was a peaceful end to the day; beautiful arrays of colors melting in the sky with a light breeze caressing her skin. If there was ever a day that Lyah wanted to disappear in the wind, today would be the day. But the more she walked, the more Lyah knew precisely what she wanted to do.

James had given her insight into her life, and for once, she felt like trying. But she needed to do it on her own. She needed to start fresh. She needed to be free, again, but different. She'd build a life—a real one this time.

"You should come to my wedding if you're going to be here tomorrow."

Lyah shook her head. "I would, but I'm only staying the night. I hope everything goes well tomorrow for you both, though."

"And I hope you find what you're looking for. I mean it. You will always hold a special place in my heart. I want the best for you."

If she were an emotional person, Lyah likely would've cried at his words. She never knew she had someone rooting for her. Someone wanting her best interests. And now she wondered if there was anyone else in her life like that.

An image of Keith popped into her head. Would he have her best interests at heart? Did he care about what happened to her after they part? Would he remember her fondly despite what she put him through?

James checked his watch. "I should get back upstairs. I told Tally I was going for a run. She'll probably start calling my phone soon."

Lyah nodded. "Yeah, I should get on my way, too."

James took her hand and held it with a sincere look in his eyes. "I'll always be here for you, Lyah. If you ever need me, please call me. I'll give you my number—"

Lyah shook her head and stepped back. "James, I can't. I mean, I won't need you. I appreciate everything. I really do. But some things should be left in the past. And with you, I'll remember where I was coming from and forget where I'm going. I can't be friends with you. Plus, you're getting married…"

"Tally knows about my past. I've told her about you."

Lyah's mouth widened. "Me? You told her about me? Why?"

"Because we don't keep secrets."

"Says the guy who told his fiancée he was going for a run."

James blushed. "Okay, so that was in bad taste, but I will tell her I ran into you. She's not the jealous type."

Lyah scuffed. "Any girl who says that is lying. Every girl is a jealous type unless they're cheating—not saying Tally is, but any other girl."

"I know Tally. She's not the jealous type."

Lyah shrugged. "If you say so."

James opened his mouth to respond, but his phone ringing interrupted him. He held up his finger to her and stepped aside so he could talk in private. Lyah spotted a bench nearby, so she went to it to sit and think as she passed the time.

Seeing James again had distracted her from her original intentions to help Keith. It was well over her twenty-minute mark. However, she wondered if Keith had time to leave. It was apparent Tally had called James by the way he was acting. Maybe Keith had finished, and she wanted James back upstairs.

Did that mean he came to his senses and decided not to go through with his plan? A delighted feeling struck her unexpectedly but quickly deflated. Keith was adamant about going through with his plan. It was unlikely he would turn back now.

But there was still the idea of Tally getting married. James seemed happy, and how James describes it, so is Tally. Did she even have unresolved feelings for Keith like James did for Lyah? Maybe, but that didn't mean Tally would drop everything for an old flame who didn't know how to let go.

Keith's plan was doomed from the start. In her heart, she knew this was a wasted trip for him, but that didn't mean it went without a wakeup call. From their talks from the last few days, his thoughts were on the fence as it was. Maybe this was his final chapter to close, much like Lyah's. The last chapter being the end of the trip.

James hung up and headed over to her. "Tally needs me back up. I guess this is goodbye?"

Lyah stood and smiled sadly with a nod. "I guess it is."

He hesitated at first but pulled her into a hug. Lyah could smell the aftershave on him and the fresh linen fragrance from his clothing. Though she wasn't sure if she should at first, she wrapped her arms around him, savoring the arms that once made her feel protected from all the evil in her world.

"I'm going to miss you. I always have," James whispered.

"I'll miss what you represented in my life at one point. You helped me in a lot of ways, and though I couldn't give you my all, I'm glad you were there for me," Lyah responded, her eyes threatening to swell with water. She left the embrace before she could get emotional and smiled. "Go to your girl, James."

He hesitated for a moment before taking her hand, squeezing it, and then letting go for the last time. "Goodbye, Lyah."

Lyah watched as he walked back into the hotel with a heavy heart. She stood there for a while, debating on her next move. Should she stay, should she wait for Keith?

Her things were in the truck, her money still accessible, and the world at her feet. Keith had brought her where she needed to be. Why prolong their goodbye anymore?

Finally, knowing what she wanted to do, she made her way to the truck. Thankfully, it was still open. She stopped for a moment, thinking of all the memories from the past week. The troubles. The running. The talks. The fights.

She would miss it all. Through it all, it felt like she had made a real friend on her journey. It was too bad it would all come to an end so soon.

Lyah gathered her things and placed them in a plastic bag she found under the seat. There was a small, tattered notebook under the seat that caught her attention. When she was done packing her things, curiosity got the best of her, and she found herself flipping through it. It was filled with notes on livestock, plants, and some chicken-scratch she could barely read. It was the truck owner's booklet. In the back were scribbles and a few numbers. There were also some blank pages.

An idea struck her, and she looked around to find a pen somewhere in the truck. Finally, she was able to find one in between the door and the passenger seat.

Lyah sat for a moment, wondering what she would say, or even if she should say anything at all. A minute passed, and at last, she found her inspiration when she saw a couple arguing near the hotel entrance.

What better way to part than to meet for the first time all over again? With a blast of memories flooding her bank, Lyah let the pen do all the talking she couldn't say as a final goodbye to Keith.

Chapter Fourteen

Keith

Keith watched Lyah as Tally's fiancé guided her into the elevator. Her face seemed off, and he got the sense they knew each other, but he knew that couldn't be right. A part of him wondered if leaving her alone with him was a good idea, but he knew she could handle herself.

That didn't stop the self-doubt from creeping into his mind, however. Their plan was flawed, that was for sure. Where he would meet with Lyah after, how they planned to part—all of it was flawed. And the gnawing feeling in the pit of his stomach was growing. He wasn't sure if it was from the prospect of meeting Tally or from leaving Lyah.

Why did he care so much?

He pushed aside the ache in his stomach and decided to stick to the plan. It was now or never. When the coast was clear, he stood in front of Tally's door, his fist positioned but frozen in his spot.

What was he waiting for?

He let out a breath and then knocked. His nerves began to kick in as the door creaked open a minute later, revealing Tally in all her glory.

Keith hadn't seen her since they parted months ago. She looked the same and yet so different. Her pin-straight hair was black with blond highlights now, and her face was dolled up, which he wasn't used to. Her dress resembled that of an American-styled kimono with red and black Japanese letters imprinted all over. Tally was always one to stay natural and wear neutral. Seeing her dressed to her finest made him take a step back.

She looked stunning.

Tally's brown eyes widened at him standing before her. She curled and uncurled her fist as if she was using her long-manicured nails to pinch herself.

"Keith? W-What are you…? How did you…?"

Keith smiled awkwardly, offering her a lame hand wave. "Hi, Tally. Can we talk?"

Tally, who was still in shock, opened the door wider for him to enter without question. Hesitantly, he brushed past her into the room, stopping short to take in his surroundings.

The room was bigger than he imagined. It looked like a studio room with the round bed centered and a jacuzzi tub next to it, but the entertainment section acted as a buffer. One floor to ceiling window and a screen door led to a balcony overlooking the city.

Keith looked to the couch and nodded towards it for Tally to sit, which she obliged. He followed soon after. Before he could start, Tally spoke, "Keith, how did you get here? How did you know I was here?"

As bad as it looked that he showed up at her door out of nowhere, he hoped she didn't take it the wrong way.

"Tally… I don't even know where to start. I have all the answers, and yet, I'm second-guessing everything," Keith admitted.

"Why don't you start by telling me why you're here. Did you come to sabotage my wedding?" There was an edge to her voice, but she remained calm.

Keith debated whether he should tell her the whole truth. He could make up a lie right then and there and be on his way. She would never have to know he came to take her back, to crash her wedding and to plead for her love. And yet when he sat there looking at her, he saw exactly what he was running from.

Expectations. A life that was molded for him and not by him. A loss of freedom. The little taste he got with Lyah was enough to make him question his entire life. Getting back with Tally would put him back to square one. Was that what he wanted?

He went for the ugly truth. "I did. I did come to sabotage your wedding. I came to tell you that I love you and that I couldn't see a life without you in it. I came to be heroic and to prove something. I came because I thought this was what I wanted."

Tally narrowed her eyes. "But?"

Keith took a deep sigh. "But this isn't what I want. I thought you were the answer to all that was wrong in my life. I thought I was saving you from making a big mistake, but it was me who was making a mistake.

"Tally, I used you without even knowing it. I thought you were it. I was hung on the idea that my coming here would fix everything. But I know that was wrong. And I'm sorry for wasting your time and my time."

Keith moved to leave, but Tally grabbed his wrist, forcing him to sit back down. "You're not going to let me talk? I have something to say."

He gave her the floor by nodding.

"I'm glad you came, Keith. While I'll admit you coming is frightening, I wondered if I was making the right decision or if my decision was based on you. For a long time, I wanted you to be where James is right now. I thought you were it. But you were lost, Keith. Everything about you screamed directionless. Yes, you had your school, you had the perfect life on the outside, but I could tell you were miserable on the inside.

"I wasn't it for you, and you weren't it for me. I realized that at some point, but you hadn't, and I needed to move on. I couldn't tell you this because you wouldn't understand.

"I struggled with the idea that I was jumping into this with James, that maybe I wasn't over you but, I realized I was stuck on trying to fix you. I wanted so bad for you to be happy, but I couldn't do that for you. You needed to do that for you. I'm glad you came because I finally can get this off my chest. But better yet, I'm glad you figured it out."

Keith sat back in shock, allowing what she said to resonate with him. It was funny how everything came full circle.

Tally moved closer, resting her hand on his knee politely. "Keith, you deserve to live the life you want. Not the life you think you need. Be spontaneous. Have fun. Do things on your own time. Your family, they care about you. But you're living for them and not for you. You deserve to be happy, too."

Tally got up to grab a drink out of the fridge. She offered him water, which he declined. Keith felt their end was drawing near, but he needed to know a few things before leaving.

When she came to stand before him, he asked, "Are you happy? Does this guy treat you well?"

Tally gave him a pleasant smile. "Yeah, I am. I'm so excited for tomorrow. I'm glad we're doing it our way. No parents, no friends. Just us. I'm making a big change in my life, and I get to do it my way. I feel… complete."

Keith nodded, a residing sadness in his heart, knowing he was about to walk away for good. But there was another part that felt like a burden had been lifted from his shoulders. "Good, you deserve everything and more."

"Would you like to stay for the wedding?"

Keith shook his head. There was only one thing on his mind tomorrow, and that involved getting to know the city of Las Vegas. Maybe with Lyah.

Lyah.

The more he stood in the room, the more he was anxious to get back to her. The urge to tell her he finally did something he felt was right. That he finally took charge for once. It was a strong feeling. Strong enough that shortly after Tally asked him to be at the wedding, he found himself out the door where he stood not too long before with shaky hands.

Tally stood with the door poised to close. “I wish you all the best, Keith. I mean that. Maybe you’ll find someone that makes you feel like they’re the right decision in your life. I hope you do.”

“Thank you, Tally. Good luck with everything.”

She closed the door, and just like that, a chapter in his life closed. Yet, it felt like a door had opened. Keith walked to the elevators with newfound purpose, and a smile etched on his face. He needed to get back to Lyah soon.

However, the smile would come to wain when he found himself lost in the sea of people checking in at the lobby. He looked around and didn’t find Lyah, then started outside, knowing he couldn’t go back inside the hotel in once he left.

But the search for her eventually turned up zilch. Then he remembered their plan to meet in the truck, and he started towards it in hopes she’d be there. He stopped midway when he noticed the truck was also empty. His steps slowed as he made his way to it. He would wait for her there as agreed.

Sliding into the truck, he immediately felt something was off. He looked around with a frown, but nothing seemed out of the ordinary, that is until his eyes landed on his duffel bag. It looked unusually thin.

Keith's heart kicked a little faster at a thought that crossed his mind. He went from fearing the worse to thinking about Lyah's history of running away. But it wasn't until he opened the bag to her clothes missing and a folded note was his suspicions confirmed.

"Lyah, why do you have to be so difficult?" Keith asked aloud as he unfolded the note.

He squeezed his eyes shut and then opened them, preparing himself for what he was about to read:

Dear Keith,

I hate your guts. Haha, no, not really. But at first, I did. In fact, a part of me still probably does for leaving me on the side of the street. But you can't blame me. You gave me hell the first couple days—no wait, that was the entire journey. Okay, I'm serious now.

Keith couldn't stop the laugh that slipped his lips. Even in letter form, she was annoying.

I wrote this letter because I hate goodbyes, and I'm never good at them (hence the whole "running away" thing). I hope things worked out for you and Tally, whatever your decision was. I met with James, and we talked, and I realized some things about myself. I may not be made for the fairytale life, but I have every bit of control of it, and I think it's time I start managing it. Yes, I'm planning on getting off the streets at some point. Maybe not today. Maybe not tomorrow. But hopefully, soon.

You've taught me a lot on this journey, but the one take away was something I never expected to experience—friendship. I can't say this to your face because I don't want you to think I'm getting soft, but I appreciate the small ounce of friendship you showed me. You're going to deny it, I'm positive. But that's exactly what you gave me, and it's exactly what I needed even though I didn't know it at the time.

Keith stopped midway, letting the memories of the week flood his bank. Who would've thought that a week's trip on the run would end up being some of the best times of his life? In another life, Keith would've never believed he'd embark on such a journey.

But our time has come to an end. You brought me to Las Vegas as promised, and you are getting the answers you need. I don't need to hold you back any longer. I'll be safe, and I'll be okay, I promise. But please do me a favor? Stop being a pussy and take control of your life, too. Go on your own adventure. Experience life for what it is while it's still here. This world is fucked, and we must squeeze out what little happiness we can.

Anyway, I'm running out of words to say, but I hope you get everything you want in life. Thank you for being there when I needed you. I'll never forget you.

Take care,
Lyah

Keith crumpled the paper and threw it on the passenger floor. He couldn't believe she would leave like that! What was he supposed to do? Drive home and call it a day?

No, he wouldn't settle for the note. After everything they'd been through, he deserved a better goodbye. Their story deserved a better ending. With newfound determination, Keith tried to start the truck.

However, after a couple of turns, the truck was stalled, and it took every ounce of energy for Keith not to scream. He sat for a moment and gathered his thoughts.

He couldn't get an Uber or Lyft without a phone, and he wouldn't be able to drive the busy streets of Las Vegas anyway with a stolen truck and cops on almost every corner. Maybe this was for the best.

Walking was out of the question, but perhaps a city bike would suffice? Keith shook his head and decided neither options were as good as taking a bus. With what he could bring and careful not to leave a trace of he or Lyah ever being in the truck including the note, Keith strapped his duffel bag on his shoulder and started for the bus stop outside the hotel.

With dusk fanning the sky, he hoped that he'd find Lyah before it was too late.

Chapter Fifteen

Keith

By morning, there was still no sign of Lyah. Keith had spent the night checking every hotel he could under the guise of looking for his missing cousin. She couldn't have gotten far considering the time of night and the dangers of the street in Sin City. He knew Lyah was smart enough to rest before heading out of town if that was her plan.

Before he knew it, midnight had come. Keith decided to call it a night and cash in on a hotel stay in the area. Most of his journey was on foot, considering the proximity of the hotels from each bus stop. He was barely a mile from where he began, but he felt like he had walked a million.

Keith was barely able to wipe the drool from the corner of his lip before he was back on his mission the next morning, having checked out and started for the hotel next door. With no sign of her there, his stomach protested for a bite to eat, and he was forced to stop at an

All-American restaurant called Oh, The Wonders.

His body drained and an impending headache catching on, Keith took a seat in the back of the restaurant and bowed his head in his hand. If he couldn't find Lyah by the end of the day, he needed another plan. He couldn't stay in Las Vegas for more than a few nights. At some point, he needed to get back to campus and face his parents. He needed to clean up his mess. His business in Vegas was done.

The waiter took his order of pancakes and orange juice, leaving him with his thoughts. The letter that he refused to throw out felt weighted in his pants pocket. A part of him felt angry that she would leave him with a letter and not a courtesy goodbye after everything they had been through.

If she had waited for him, he would've dropped her anywhere she wanted. He was in no hurry to get home and deal with his parents and school. Did their time together mean so little to her? Why did it bother him so much?

The waiter came back with his food, and Keith took a bite, savoring the feel of pancake fluff and syrup on his tongue with his eyes closed. When he opened them, he jumped back in his seat, nearly choking on the food he hadn't yet fully swallowed.

Lyah appeared like a figment of his imagination across from him, her hands clasped and a daring smile on her face.

"What the fuck, Lyah!" Keith choked out in between coughs. A few heads turned in Keith's direction in disapproval, but he ignored them. "What are you doing here?"

"I should be asking you that same question," Lyah countered. She leaned over to grab a pancake from his plate, but he slapped her hand away. "Are you following me?"

Keith took a sip of his orange juice to clear his throat. "Following? I've been *searching* for you since last night! Why the hell would you leave like that?"

Lyah rolled her eyes. "Did you see my note? I explained everything."

"No. I mean, yes, I saw the note. No, you did not explain everything. Did you completely forget that there is a possible madman on the loose looking for us?" Keith whispered the last part with his head bowed to not alert the people around them.

"Yes, and you obviously didn't read between the lines of the letter. I will handle it. There's no reason for you to come after me. With you gone, there is one less person to put in danger. He wants me, not you."

"Lyah, listen to me. I could care less for my safety at this point. We've been through so much to get here, and you just leave me with a lousy note with a lousy excuse?"

Lyah's mouth was open in shock. "Oh my gosh."

Keith looked at her with wide eyes, wondering why she was looking at him like that. "What?"

A slow smile formed on her face. "You came to find me because you missed me, and you didn't get to say goodbye."

Keith stared at her, shaking his head in denial. He looked like a deer caught in headlights. "No. No! That has nothing to do with it. Lyah, you shouldn't be alone—"

"You missed me."

"No, I didn't."

"Yes, you did!"

"Lyah, no—"

"Just admit it already! You're mad I left the note, and you didn't get to say goodbye, and it's irking you, so you came looking for me to tell me that you miss me, and you don't want our journey together to end."

Keith sat back in silence and defiance. She was right, but he wasn't going to admit it to her. That smug look on her face had him rethinking everything he did. He should've gone home.

"It's dangerous out here for you, Lyah. For us. We need to resolve this thing with that guy before I can go home. I can't go back knowing that you're still out here, and I didn't do anything to help."

Lyah twiddled her thumbs as she digested his words. It was the first time he was able to get a good look at her since she sat. She looked… normal. Normal as in, fresh and properly clothed. Her dark curls were in pigtails around her shoulders, and she had on a white t-shirt and skinny black jeans. They were likely apart of the pile they picked up at the thrift store not too long ago. Her face was void of any manipulations. A far cry from the night he met her but a look he'd grown to like.

"We may be in luck."

"What?"

"He called my hotel room and—"

"He called your hotel room? How the hell did he find you? Better yet, how did you get a hotel room without an ID?" So many questions swirled in his head.

Lyah narrowed her eyes at him. "Can you let me finish? After I 'borrowed' a girl's ID from a bar, I got a room at a nearby hotel. He called me as soon as I stepped out of the shower. I have no idea how he knew I was there.

"Anyway, he called and told me if I didn't come up with ten grand in eight hours to replenish his 'stock,' he says I wouldn't want to find out what he has in store for us."

"How are you sure it's him?" Keith asked. His nerves were rattled. Now he knew for sure they were being followed.

"I recognized his voice, though his accent was gone. I suspected it was a fake after the motel incident. I told him I'd add interest if he agreed to leave you alone."

Keith didn't know what to say at first. Where were they going to find that amount of money in such a short time? "Why would you do that? I'm not letting you do this alone, Lyah. If he wants the money, we'll get it together. And why eight hours from now? Where does he want us to leave the money if we even get it?" Keith didn't want to think about what kind of troubled they'd be if they didn't.

Lyah shrugged. "He wants to meet at some abandoned magic theatre. I think it's across town. I'm not sure why he's giving us eight hours, though."

Maybe he was still on his way to Vegas. If that were the case, who was watching them? Keith shifted his gaze around the restaurant. No one was paying them any mind.

"Did you know his name is Charlie? What kind of bad guy is named Charlie?"

"You should've known that from the moment you two met!"

Lyah rolled her eyes. "I was only after one thing. If he told me his name, I wasn't listening."

"So, what were you calling him before?"

"Target #32."

Keith rubbed his forehead in defeat. "So, how do we go about this? Where are we getting ten grand—plus interest—to hand over in a few hours?"

"We can do this the old-fashioned way."

Keith quirked an eyebrow. "Which is…?"

"A good old-fashioned target hunt!" Lyah said with glee.

"You mean—"

"Yep, the Artisan way."

Keith sighed. That might be their only option, though… "How much do you have left?"

Lyah mentally calculated. "Based on the hotel stay last night, the clothes, food… Maybe $1,100."

Keith groaned. Maybe he could… no, he couldn't. He wouldn't. Crap. "How about I spot the rest?"

Lyah looked at him in bewilderment. “What? No! I’m not going to let you do that.”

“Lyah, we have to.”

“No! That’s like, stealing from you.”

“What’s the difference? You do it to others.”

“The difference is it’s you!” Keith drew silent as Lyah tried to look for the right words to say. “Keith, I meant what I said in that letter. We don’t know each other extremely well, yet I feel like you’re the closest friend I’ve ever had. You’ve helped me in more ways than I could’ve ever imagined, and I’m grateful for that. I’ve never had someone go all out for me, not even James. I didn’t want to bring you down further than you already have for me.”

Keith just remembered something. “Wait, the guy yesterday and in the letter—Tally’s fiancé—was that—”

“Yeah. It was. Small world.”

“Wow.” His suspicions about them knowing each other were right. Now he was more curious about what they talked about, but he decided against asking. Hearing Lyah pour her heart out like she had in the letter stirred something in his stomach.

The waiter came to take Keith’s half-eaten plate of food, but Lyah shooed him away and grabbed it instead. Unapologetically, she ate the remaining bits, leaving Keith in awe.

“So, off-topic, how did things go with Tally?” Lyah asked with her mouth full.

Keith scrunched his nose but answered, “It went well, I guess.

We talked and cleared the air, and she gave me some perspective. I left feeling like I have all the answers I needed."

Lyah nodded. "I'm glad you came to your senses."

"What?" Keith asked in confusion.

"Tally was never what you wanted. Tally was a pre-conceived expectation. It wasn't her you wanted, so-to-speak. It was the idea of her."

Keith figured that out. "What about you and James? Did you get answers?"

"Plenty. Once this whole shebang is over, I'm going to take another shot at life."

Keith smiled. He was genuinely glad she was taking her lifestyle into consideration. "I'm glad to hear that."

Lyah finished the plate and motioned the waiter to take it though he looked more annoyed than anything. Lyah paid him no mind and turned back to Keith.

"So, what do we do now? I hope this doesn't get in the way of you going back home."

"I'm not going home until this Charlie guy is taken care of." And there wasn't a thing she could say to change his mind. She must've sensed it too because she didn't try to fight him on it.

"You said you wanted to help me," Lyah began. "Where are you going to find that kind of money?"

"I have a savings account that my parents control, but I have the information for it. If they haven't locked it by now, we can take out what we need and then be on our way."

"Why would they lock it if it's technically yours?" Lyah asked.

Because with him not obeying their every command, they wouldn't think he's fit to handle anything else. They've threatened to take his savings on more than one occasion just for not attending a class or two. "Because they're my parents." It was all he needed to say.

"And if it's locked?"

Keith grinned. "Then, we do it the Artisan way."

Lyah thought for a moment, likely wrestling with the idea of having Keith on board to help get Charlie off their backs. "Okay, if we're going to do this, we need to do it sooner than later."

"Agreed," Keith said. "But we still have a problem."

"What problem?" Lyah looked confused.

"There's obviously someone following us. And if it's who I think it is, then we need to be extra careful."

"The bald guy you mentioned?"

Keith nodded. "If he's not with Charlie, then he's in the shadows, and we can't afford to let our guards down. He's tracking us somehow. Maybe he never stopped following us after the crash."

Lyah asked, "Then what do we do? We can't shake a ghost."

"No, we can't. But we can be mindful of what we do and say. He might have his own instructions that Charlie failed to mention to you. Just be careful."

Lyah nodded and looked outside the window. "It's going to rain soon. We should do this before it slows us down."

"Then let's go find an ATM."

Keith dropped a few bills on the table and got up with his duffel bag and Lyah in tow. On the way out of the restaurant, she told him she wanted to check out of her hotel next door first and left to get her things.

And to think he was so close to finding her on his own.

She returned half an hour later with a bag of clothes and supplies that she had taken the day before from Keith's duffel bag. Just outside the restaurant, Lyah stopped abruptly, swinging her head from side-to-side. "Um, where's the truck?"

"It stalled at the hotel where Tally's staying. It was probably for the best considering we're on city streets, and it's practically crowded with cops."

Lyah groaned. "We have to walk everywhere? Can't we Uber? Lyft?"

"With what phone?"

"Good point."

***

"Locked. Just like I thought."

"You've got to be kidding me…"

"I wish I was," Keith said as he banged his head against the ATM. "They're going to flag the account now, I'm sure of it. They're going to know where I am, what happened to the wagon, and likely bring hell to me. But you what? Fuck it!"

Lyah drew closer, concerned. "Are you okay?"

"Dandy. I guess we're down to Plan B. I hope you know what you're doing."

"It's all I know."

Keith banged his head again with a groan. "We're so fucked."

"What happened to that enthusiasm in the restaurant?" Lyah crossed her arms over her chest, her head cocked to the side as she revered him.

"That was before I had time to register the consequences of this. If I use the cash on me now, I probably won't be able to make it home and get the wagon. It's likely already at the pound." There was so much more wrong considering he never reported the car stolen, and his parents were likely already notified if the car was found. They'd either think he was dead and someone's using his account or that he was on the loose and had lost his mind.

Either way, he would be in deep trouble when he got back home but not just with his parents.

"Don't you have another account?"

"If they froze this one, they froze the others. The cash I have I can't give to you. I need it to go home or at best, for another hotel stay."

"Damn it. Where's the nearest casino?"

"Casino?" Keith stepped away from the ATM to let the woman behind him use it. The woman threw him a dirty look before doing her business.

"Maybe we can flip what I have before we try target practice," Lyah suggested. It wasn't the worst idea, but his luck in gambling was trash. Either way, it might solve their issue faster.

"How's your luck?" he asked.

"Probably better than yours, not that it matters," she mumbled. Lyah looked around and spotted one two blocks away on the corner. "Let's see if that one is open," she motioned to the sign that read Dune Valley Casino.

"Casinos are always open. Let's get this over with." Keith started for the casino but stopped when he realized Lyah wasn't following. "Are you coming?"

Lyah looked sheepish. "We have a problem."

Keith cast her a dark look. "Problem? That's all we seem to have lately. What is it now?"

"The fake ID I swiped last night is of an 18-year-old. And even if I had my real one, I wouldn't be able to get in."

It took him a moment to register what she was saying. His eyes enlarged when he figured it out. "You mean, you're not 21?" Keith wasn't sure why he hadn't asked before. He knew she was younger than him, but how young?

Lyah brushed his surprise aside. "No, I'm not. At least not for another three months. My custom fake ID was left in my motel room before… well, you know."

Keith dragged his hand down his face. "So, I'm going in by

myself?" The thought made him queasy. He was fine with going into a casino on his own, but the pressure of trying to gamble for the situation they were in made him nervous. This would not end well.

"Not quite. It's up to you. But I can't sneak into a heavily guarded casino or charm my way through the door. I'm skilled, but not that skilled."

"Crap!" Keith tried to think of another option. "What about your old methods? Why don't you just steal another ID?"

"Shhh!" Lyah drew him closer by the sleeve of his shirt to make sure those walking by hadn't heard him. "That's not something you want to blurt out, Keith."

Keith held his hands up in surrender. "I'm sorry! But we need to think of something."

"I can't take another ID that doesn't look like me. It's one thing to use it in a leisure hotel and another in a guarded place like a casino. They look a whole lot harder at these things in casinos. Trust me, I've tried in the past, and I nearly had the cops called on me."

"Then maybe we shouldn't do the casino thing. If I go into the casino and lose all the money, we're doomed. Maybe we should stick to the original plan, after all." He hated that they had to. If only his account wasn't locked, all their issues would be solved.

Lyah frowned. "I don't know, Keith. It's not that simple. If you're not comfortable doing this, this plan could fail, too. Plus, I'm completely out of my element. It's about knowing the area and how the people are. You have to study people, and that takes time we don't have."

"I thought you were confident at the restaurant," Keith said, throwing her words back at her.

Lyah glared at him. "I am. But the more I think about it, the more it sounds like a bad idea. This isn't my territory, and it takes time to get to know the people in the area for me to maneuver freely. Not to mention, this isn't the backwoods of Pennsylvania. Security cameras are everywhere. I can't pickpocket if I wanted."

She looked as if she was struggling with the idea. But Keith knew the moment she resigned to it when her shoulders sagged in defeat. This would be their all or nothing plan. And it could very well get them arrested or killed if they weren't careful.

"We can try this, Lyah. Uncomfortable or not, it's the only choice we have now. Let's spend the rest of the day finding a good target and then strike or, however you want to do this."

Lyah looked shocked but then smiled. "I'm surprised you would push for this."

"Why because it doesn't fit your 'nerd' persona of me? We don't have a choice."

Lyah nodded. "Actually, yes."

Keith turned on his heel and started walking down the street ahead of her, his long strides making her struggle to keep up. Why he asked that question, he didn't know, but the answer dug at him for whatever reason, as childish as it was.

"Did I hurt your feelings? Why are you walking away?" Lyah

called after him. There was less mockery in her tone than curiosity.

"I'm going to prove you wrong."

"Prove me wrong?"

Keith stopped abruptly, causing Lyah to crash into him. She rubbed her nose with a frown but said nothing. "Yes, prove you wrong. I'm not a nerd. I can do bad things, too."

Lyah squinted at him and then burst out in laughter. Keith folded his arms with a scowl on his face, not finding it funny. His image may not scream "bad boy," but he was ready to take the necessary risks to help his friend.

Friend.

Lyah was his friend.

The revelation was startling, and he found himself loosening his arms, his scowl turning into a slow grin, and eventually laughter. When tears started forming in his eyes as Lyah doubled over, he couldn't help but think this was the best feeling in the world, and he never wanted it to go away.

Lyah, who was still giggling, grabbed his hand and walked forward. "Come on, 'bad boy.' I'll show you how it's really done."

Chapter Sixteen

Lyah

Lyah couldn't believe he came looking for her. Keith was a lot of things, and passionate was one of those; she came to learn. It was nice to know she fell under that umbrella.

Seeing him in the restaurant had thrown her for a loop. After spending the night in the hotel next door, Lyah had decided to catch breakfast on the way out. She had no particular plans to leave the city yet as she hadn't mapped out her next steps, but she wanted to put some distance between her and Keith.

So much for that plan.

The minute she saw him sit at his table with a plate of breakfast, her legs had drawn her to him anyway.

Her priorities were not in order, she admitted. With the phone call she received the night before from Charlie, she should've been more rattled. The truth was, she was more scared not having Keith by her side. But it wasn't for protection.

She had contemplated if she was making the right choice, leaving him behind. It seemed fate had its own plan. Perhaps this was her opportunity to set things right before she decided to lead a life of the narrow and straight. To move on, she needed to right her wrongs starting with Charlie and help clear Keith from her mess. Once they found a way to pay him back and clear their names, Lyah would be on her way. This time with a clear conscience.

Keith and Lyah spent most of the day people watching in different settings, Lyah going over who to watch and who not to. It was a skill that not many could accomplish. To find the right target, the observer needed to know them from afar. One had to read their movements and their personality traits from handling things like a cigarette or confrontation. How they reacted to being in a crowd. It was often hard to gauge their mannerisms and personalities in a non-social setting. Naturally, a bar or club was the best way to find a target. It was a lot easier to figure out whether the target had money once they started talking.

In broad daylight, it was usually the worst time to find the kind of target she needed. But in the city of Las Vegas, where the streets never rested, and most social places were never closed, it was easy to find what they needed.

Instead of jumping straight into it, Lyah decided to teach Keith about people. They had a few hours to kill before meeting Charlie, and if they pulled this off correctly, they only needed to make one hit to meet their goal.

"What about that guy? He looks loaded," Keith said, pointing to a guy in an expensive-looking suit who was sitting down at the bar they decided to scout.

Lyah shook her head. "No, he's not the one."

"Why not? He might be worth the shot."

"There's a couple things wrong with him being a target." Keith sat back and listened attentively. "First of all, he's not loaded. That suit he has on is rented."

Keith frowned as he took another look at the guy. "How do you know that?"

"He rolled the sleeved up to drink. A man with money wouldn't care if it got stained because he can afford to clean or replace it unless he's a neat freak. Second, there's a tag sticking out at the bottom, and the way he's looking around makes me think he wants people to think he has money. He's trying to pick up a lady. Or a man if he swings that way."

"Oh," Keith huffed and sat back with his arms crossed.

"But his next seat neighbor might do the trick." Lyah pointed with her chin to the guy who was carefully nursing a beer in his hand. The guy appeared to be an average Joe from the outside, but there was something else there. Lyah's eyed the watch on his right hand, complementing his otherwise ordinary jeans and yellow shirt. She had seen one of those watches before on a target back in New Jersey. She came to learn it was an old-money watch, one that wasn't made anymore but still held weight.

Lyah didn't know enough about watches to know the exact kind or how old it really was, but she did know the type of people to wear it. A few of her wealthiest targets had one just like it. She eyed the man with his legs crossed and the tapping of his finger against the wine-colored counter. His head swinging in perfect synchronization with the young bartender as he shifted from patron to patron. She was getting a vibe…

"I think you should do this one," Lyah said to Keith.

He looked at her incredulously. "What? No! I know nothing about this. I thought I would only be watching?"

"You said you wanted to help. What happened to the 'bad boy' showing me he's got it? Go strike up a conversation with him."

Keith shook his head, feverishly. "Lyah, I can't. I crumble when it counts the most. What am I supposed to say? What if I say the wrong thing?"

Lyah grabbed Keith by the shoulders in reassurance. "Just be natural."

"I don't know what natural is."

"Then pretend to act like me," Lyah countered. She would not let him bail from their little project though important it may be. If this were to be the last entertainment she ever saw, she'd be okay with it. A drop of sweat hit the table from his forehead as he got up tentatively to sit next to the man.

Lyah suppressed a giggle as she watched Keith stumble to find the right words. Eventually, it seemed he got a hold of himself after ordering a beer and relaxing back.

She couldn't hear exactly what they were saying though she could assume from their gestures, the man seemed to be enjoying their conversation as he continued leaning in, his eyes had yet to leave Keith's moving mouth. It was so easy for guys to talk to each other. They could literally pick a topic from thin air and have a great time.

Lyah envied that. The women she encountered were always standoffish, but perhaps for a good reason given her chosen line of work.

Lyah took a sip of her orange soda Keith kindly bought for her. She sat amused as she observed the man's position, fully attentive to Keith, a permanent smile etched on his face, the constant need to grab Keith's shoulder as he spoke.

Lyah couldn't control the laughter that burst through her mouth, causing several people to turn to her in confusion, including Keith and his new *friend*. Keith's eyebrows knitted, and then discretely, he gestured to the restroom in the back. He got up first, then Lyah followed.

When they met up in the hall, Keith looked around the corner to ensure no one was in the vicinity. "Okay, I got a problem. He wants to meet up at a casino later."

Another laugh threatened to escape, but Lyah did her best to reign it in. "Then, go. Once he withdraws cash, you take it, and we're on our way."

"This seems way too easy. There's no way he's got ten grand to blow."

"Fifteen grand, and that's because it is too easy," Lyah said. "We're in Vegas. There's no telling what stupid things people will blow their money on."

Keith wasn't satisfied with that answer. "But how do I get it in my hand? And how do I convince him to just hand over that much? Do I steal it and run? What if he doesn't have that much?"

Lyah tried to catch each of his questions. He was nervous. The sweat building back on his forehead was evidence enough. "I can't predict his moves or what he has in the bank, but I trust my gut when I say he's our guy. You'll know what to do when the time comes. You'll be in a casino filled with people,"—and security cameras— "there's plenty of people to talk to or slip some cash from."

Lyah had a feeling it would be easy pickings for Keith, but just in case, she would scout while he's in the casino though she wouldn't let him in on that detail.

Keith pressed his lips. "That's the vaguest statement ever. I know nothing about this business. That's the advice you have for a newbie?"

Lyah ignored his question. "What time does he want to meet up?"

"He wants to meet up at 7 p.m. That's too close to our time with Charlie. Maybe I can push him to go earlier." He was right about the time, but if their target was as fruitful as her gut was telling her, they could get what they needed in the time frame. Granted, the whole plan was dependent on Keith not chickening out.

Lyah waved him off. "We'll be fine. It shouldn't take any more than thirty minutes to get what we need. Obviously, I can't go in, but you've got this. We'll rehearse different scenarios before then to prepare you. Besides, I get the impression if you asked for it, he'll probably just hand it to you."

Keith asked, "What makes you say that?"

He hadn't caught on. Lyah stifled a grin. "Never mind. Just go for it. He's our best shot right now. Did he say what casino he wanted to go to? I hope it's close."

"I convinced him to stay in the area. I told him I've never been to a casino. He's going to show me the ropes."

Lyah bit her lip to keep from smiling. She couldn't help herself. But if their target was willing to spend the evening splurging with a stranger, things might work for them yet. "I'm sure he will. Now, go back before he suspects something."

Keith was about to leave but regarded her carefully. "Is there something you're not telling me?"

"No, why?"

Keith paused, then shook his head. "Don't bother. I don't think I want to know." She waited until he was out of earshot before doubling over once again, this time having all the fun to herself.

***

It would take hours before the crucial night descended upon them. Keith was jittery as usual, Lyah still keeping her inside jokes to herself. When they got outside the casino doors their target had agreed to meet, Keith turned to her, his eyes shifting up and down the street in caution.

"Lyah, what if I don't do this in time? If I get this done at the last minute, we'll still need time to get to where we need to go. And we can't be late."

No, they couldn't. After spending the day trying to scout and seeing no other targets Lyah could discretely take on, this was their last shot at getting what they needed. Granted, as the clock wore down, Lyah found her concentration shot, and her chances of helping their situation had depleted when she couldn't find anyone else to target. "We're covered. You got this, Keith. I know you do. Now go before you waste time."

"Right… What's the plan, again?"

"Keith!"

"I know, I know! I just want to make sure my bases are covered," Keith said as he rubbed his hands on his pants.

Lyah pinched her nose with a sigh. "When you meet him, convince him to withdraw the amount we need. If he has it, great. If he doesn't, get as close to the amount as possible. There's time to double or triple that amount if you're lucky.

"Once he does that, you follow him to a machine or table, and you watch him until he's completely emerged in the game or inebriated or whatever you do to get him distracted from his pockets or convince him to let you hold it. You take his wallet and cash, slip it into your pocket, go to the bathroom, and then slip out when the coast is clear. Got it?"

"And if that doesn't work?."

"That's plan A. If that goes wrong, go with plan B and C like we discussed. Either risk taking his credit card and withdrawing it yourself or find someone else you can easily slip money from like an old lady or something. Beyond that, you're on your own. Make up a sob story or something. He looks sensitive enough to believe it. And don't be above begging and making false promises. People are as dumb as they look to fall for it. But something tells me this may be an easy win for us."

Keith stepped back. "What do you mean? Come to think of it, you've been hinting at something since I met this guy. What are you not telling me?"

Lyah eyes turned into slits. "Now is not the time, Keith. Hurry up and go in!"

"Just tell me!"

Lyah tried to school her features and remain stoic, but it wasn't happening. She turned to hide her smile. He wasn't going to leave until she told him. She hoped this didn't hinder their plans. With resolve, she turned back around and said, "He's probably gay."

Keith's mouth opened in shock. "What? Wait, does he think this is a date?!"

"No time, Keith. Go in!" Lyah practically dragged him to the door in protest, letting him enter without another word.

Such a stubborn man, she thought.

Letting Keith take charge would either make or break their situation. But she couldn't doubt him now. This plan had to work, as flawed as it was. But she was desperate. She made a promise the night before that if she could get through this little stubble, she would never steal again if it didn't pertain to life or death.

Perched on the bus bench yards from the casino, Lyah watched as people excitedly went about their business on the strip. They were tourists if their pointing, and random pictures of the dazzling light shows from the surrounding buildings were anything to go by. Oh, how she wished she could explore the area on a night as such.

Though judging from the low rumblings in the cloud cover, there wouldn't be much excitement in a few. The bus bench held no shelter, so by the time it had begun to drizzle, Lyah picked up Keith's duffel bag with her stuff once again inside and found cover under a canopy of a closed flower shop nearby.

The strip had thinned and soon became bare when the rain began to pelt the ground. Arms crossed and foot-tapping, Lyah felt useless having to stand around and not be the star of the show. But she prayed Keith could handle himself and be the real winner of the night, granted he was the one ultimately saving her life when it really mattered. Again.

Movement from the corner of her eye caught her attention, and she straightened when she noticed a bald man in a dark coat standing near the entrance of an alleyway nearby.

No cigarette, phone, or even an umbrella in hand, Lyah wondered what he was doing standing there. She would soon get her answer when he craned his neck and stared right at her.

Her heart leapt into her throat, the action catching her off guard. He was still staring, no smile or frown on his face, just an emotionless stare. Why wasn't he looking away? Why wasn't she?

A shiver crept down her spine, and she forced herself to look away, but curiosity got the best of her, and she couldn't help but turn back to him. He was still there and still staring, paying no mind to the rain bouncing off his coat or his shiny head.

Bald guy… Was it the guy Keith had mentioned from the thrift store? Did he work for Charlie? Had he come for her?

As the questions swirled and alarm bells rang internally, Lyah urged her feet to move, rain or no rain. She needed to get away from him as soon as possible. Swiftly, Lyah started in the opposite direction and past the casino. Anxiously, she glanced at the entrance, willing Keith to come out any minute. She wouldn't know when or where to meet him with no phone if she had to get from the area.

Daringly, Lyah glanced behind her as she made it past the casino doors, hoping the man had forgotten about her and left. Her knees nearly buckled when she saw him following her, closer than he was before, his stare still penetrating her with a dead gaze.

She picked up her steps and kept forward. If she could cross the street or take a shortcut somewhere and lose him in a crowd, she could probably make it back to the casino as if nothing happened.

She breathed a sigh of relief when she was able to cross the street with a small crowd of people with umbrellas. By now, her clothes were completely soaked, her hair drenched, and her shoes making squishing noises as she walked, but she paid no mind.

Taking a left, a right, and another right, Lyah was finally able to find a sea of people with umbrellas standing outside a venue waiting for what, she wasn't sure. She looked back as she tumbled through the crowd, having not seen the bald man anywhere near her. Taking it a bit further, she faked a left on another block, and there, she finally felt she could rest.

The street wasn't crowded. In fact, it was nearly empty. But the bald guy was nowhere to be found, and that was all that mattered. Lyah breathed a sigh of relief, her heart finally catching up with her nerves, and she leaned against the window of a closed coffee shop near an alleyway.

Her leisure didn't last long.

The sound of screeching tires brought her out of her stupor, and Lyah had no time to react as the back door of a black truck swung open, two beefy guys stepping out and approaching her with quick steps.

Lyah fumbled as one grabbed her in a semi-chokehold and covered her mouth, the scream at the back of her throat muted. She banged on the man's arms as the other man took her feet and held them up as she struggled to get loose in their arms.

Carrying her to the truck, Lyah used her foot to avoid being pushed in by stiffening it on the door frame. She wrestled the man's hand off her mouth, and she managed a scream before her mouth was covered again.

As a last-ditch effort, she bit his palm as best she could, eliciting an angry growl from the dark man. Without warning, he punched her in the head, her limbs falling limp, and they both tossed her into the truck face first.

As she lay dazed, she could hear the door to the other side open and close. She was forced to sit up as the men slid in beside her, caging her between them. Her head rolled to the side, a massive headache fogging her brain and an impending throb at her temple.

She could feel the truck move as she struggled to keep her eyes open. There was a man up front in the passenger seat next to another driving. The last thing she could remember before drifting off was the man in the passenger seat, turning around to look at her, a sinister smile spread across his lips.

"Sweet dreams, Lyah. I can't wait to be the last face you will ever see."

The southern drawl was most certainly gone. The man before her was not the man she met at the bar in Pennsylvania. Not the drunken klutz who paid for her motel room and fell asleep seconds after entering. Not a target who had fallen into her grasp, whose remaining money still weighed heavy in her pocket.

No, this was someone worse. Someone she had the misfortune of taking advantage of. This was the real Charlie.

Chapter Seventeen

Keith

By now, Keith had bailed on plans A and B, and Plan C was not something he was looking forward to. The more he got to know the guy from the bar—Ian—the more he felt dirty and wrong. How did Lyah do this so often? But he needed a quick alternative. If they were to survive the night, he needed to make this work.

Keith was sitting at a table, watching Ian dominate the game in front of him. As it turned out, Ian had already withdrawn money and was playing with cash on hand, cash Keith had yet to see in its entirety. How much Ian was sitting on was a mystery at this point, and Keith couldn't bring himself to pickpocket to find out.

Keith had sat out the last three games with the excuse of not knowing how to play to avoid using the cash he had. He didn't want to risk losing it all at a game he knew he couldn't win with his luck.

Ian had noticed Keith's reclusiveness and avoidance and turned to him with a frown of his own. "Keith, what's wrong? You've been off since we got here."

Keith couldn't face him. "It's nothing. I'm enjoying myself."

Ian stared at him and then turned back to the dealer, "Can you excuse me for a sec?"

Ian surprised Keith by taking his hand and giving him his undivided attention. Keith's eyes widened, and he was about to yank his hand from him but then remembered what Lyah said. If Ian had taken a liking to him and was concerned, perhaps this could work for him yet. "What's wrong? You can tell me. Maybe I can help."

What sob story could he come up with? Lying wasn't his thing, but he needed to fast. Then, a light bulb went off in his head. Why not stretch the truth?

Keith took on a forlorn look. "It's my cousin… Lila. She's in big trouble."

"What kind of trouble?"

Keith pretended to sniff. Was he overdoing it? Perhaps. "She got into some trouble with a gang. You see, her mother—my aunt—is dying of cancer, and to pay the medical bills, she had to… turn to the streets.

"She had to borrow some money from a gang to keep afloat and to ensure her mother survived, but the gang wants repayment tonight; otherwise, they will… it's too hard to think about."

Ian's mouth formed an O. "Oh, my! What about your other family members? Can't they help?"

Keith shook his head, "We're all that's left. Cancer runs through the family."

Ian rubbed his thumb over Keith's hand. Keith struggled not to react and pull it away in discomfort. "I'm so sorry! Is there any way I can help?"

Was this the moment of truth? Was he supposed to say what he needed, or should he milk the situation some more?

"I don't know…" Keith found himself saying. "I was hoping that coming here, I might be able to turn a profit for her, but I'm terrified to spend what little I have and lose everything. I shouldn't have come. But I might lose her and not to mention my aunt would be devastated—"

"How much do you need?"

The words got caught in his throat. Was Ian about to do it? There's was no way Ian would fall for it. Keith braced himself for disappointment at the thought he could walk away with nothing tonight, and he and Lyah would really be dead.

Keith decided to give it a shot anyway. "Twenty thousand." For any more interest that might happen to come upon Charlie's end.

Ian gripped his hand a little tighter, either because the amount was so large or because he felt anger towards Keith's fake story, Keith wasn't sure. Ian pursed his lips. "I don't have that amount—" Keith sagged his shoulders, "—but my boyfriend does, and I happen to have his card tonight."

Keith perked up, thinking his ears had failed him. "Come again?" Wait, boyfriend?

Ian smiled. "I'll help you because you seem genuine, and honestly, I was just going to blow half that amount here as payback for him flirting with that slick-hair cat freak that lives in the studio below us. He's loaded and probably won't miss it anyway."

"Y-You're going to help me?" Keith was still in shock. Lyah was right.

He could hear her voice in the back of his head, "*I'm always right!*"

"Of course! Now, let's head to the counter. I hear they do cash advances here, and you can probably walk right out with it. Think of it as my one good deed for the year. But I do ask for a tiny favor."

Uh oh. Keith held his breath.

Ian leaned in close, too close with a flirty smile. "Let's do this again sometime, eh?"

Keith tried not to shrink away. There was no way in hell, but he could only manage a nod before Ian released his hand and got up from the table, his game long forgotten. "If the cash advance doesn't do it, then we make our way to another table and double what we got. Casinos are my thing, so you have nothing to worry about. How much time do you have to make this drop?"

Keith spied a clock on the wall. Crap, they barely had thirty minutes left. "Before 8 p.m., if necessary."

“Then, let’s make this count, shall we?” Ian threw him a wink and hurried to the counter. Keith could only tag behind, his sweat and worry trailing behind him.

***

He couldn’t believe it was that easy. There was no way. It had to be a dream. Keith could only stand on the slick sidewalk, his pocket weighted with cash, and his mouth still hanging open.

With time to spare, he had really saved the day. He couldn’t wait to tell Lyah. She would be so proud. But where was she? Keith’s shock dulled when he looked up and down the street, Lyah nowhere to be seen.

Keith ran a hand down his face. He had told her to stay put but knowing her, she had gotten hungry or was likely targeting someone herself. Regardless, now was not the time to be on a hunt for Lyah with their limited time frame.

He walked left, then right outside the casino, passing a few pedestrians who were closing their umbrellas as the rain had finally come to a stop. Where could she be? She couldn’t have gotten very far.

Or maybe something happened to her? Keith shook the thoughts from his head. Though he did warn her before, the streets were busy tonight. There was no way someone could harm her in a place like this. It was too risky.

Unless…

Keith groaned as he did a full circle around the strip. If he went too far and she came back, he risked wasting more time. But if she was nearby and had forgotten about their time limit, he could be on his way. And then there was that third option. If something really did happen to her… his stomach dropped at the thought.

Charlie wouldn't, right? Not without his money. It wouldn't make sense for him to take her. But as he craned his neck around and found those dark empty eyes staring right back at him, he knew Charlie could and Charlie would.

"Oh, fuck." It was the bald guy staring right at him from a parked black truck on the side of the road. How long had he been there staring at him? Watching him lose his mind?

Without thinking, Keith took a step forward, then several more until he was almost face-to-face with the bald man. He looked even scarier up close. Did he even blink? His voice shaky, Keith asked, "W-What did you do with Lyah?" Never mind Keith's boldness to approach the guy, something his feet had decided without his permission but had he accused a relatively dangerous stranger of kidnapping or harming his friend?

Twenty grand suddenly made him invincible, it seemed.

The bald man, who smelled of leather and pinewood, stepped from the black truck toward Keith, who took a giant step back. He tried to ignore the sudden loss of balance and squared his shoulders though it was a futile effort.

The bald man bent down, their eyes leveled, and said in a gruff voice, “Charlie awaits you at the destination.”

He turned and opened the back door. Was he supposed to get in? Keith saw this ending badly in several different ways. But Charlie was the wrong dude to cross—again—and he obviously was expecting him. Had he picked up Lyah, too? Was that why she wasn’t waiting for him outside the casino?

The bald man was not one to talk, and it would be wasteful to ask any more questions. Without further instruction, Keith hopped into the back of the truck, the door frighteningly closing after him.

This could end one of two ways, and Keith wasn’t sure which option meant an escape. Either way, he hoped Lyah was okay. If luck was on her side, she really had decided to get ice cream or a plate of food and escaped the clutches of Charlie. Once the money was out of his pocket and in Charlie’s hand, he hoped this whole thing could be behind them.

The bald man hopped into the driver seat and started the truck, and along on their journey they went. Keith wondered why the bald man made no attempt to blindfold him like he saw in movies. Wouldn’t it be wise for Keith not to know where they were going?

But this wasn’t a movie, which could mean he wouldn’t live to tell anyone else about it. Keith shuttered at the thought. Many questions swirled in Keith’s head, but he clamped his mouth shut, trusting his gut to keep quiet around the man upfront. If his stoically closed-off persona were any indication, he most certainly was not one to mess with, let alone hope to get answers from.

It didn't take any more than twenty minutes before the truck pulled up at an abandoned theater called The Magic Stage. Was this the destination Lyah had mentioned earlier?

By now, it was well past their time limit. Keith wondered if their drive to the destination would factor into the meeting. The bald man parked, stepped out of the truck, opened Keith's door, and led him into the building without another word.

The building was dark at the entrance, but beyond the halls where they walked through to the theater were bright lights centered on a stage, an audience of four in the seats.

Keith stopped dead in his tracks as he realized who they were and what was going on. Up on stage, bound by rope with her hands behind her back, and her clothes soaked was Lyah. A nasty bruise could be seen at her temple, and she laid on the floor, unmoving. Too still.

Keith sucked in a breath. What had they done to her? What were they going to do to her? Was she still alive?

"Nice of you to finally join us."

Keith's head swung to the voice, recognizing the man sitting at the front row, three unknown men at his side. The bald guy took his place behind Keith, nodding him forward until he was front and center. If his legs hadn't given out before, they sure were likely to now.

This was not the same drunk man he found shooting out his car window in Pennsylvania. The man before him was different, more sophisticated, and curter. His slight accent was gone, and his outfit screamed mafia boss.

Charlie was in the flesh.

“Miss me?” Charlie asked as he took a stand in front of Keith. The bald guy took his position beside the other three. “I believe you have something for me?”

“Not until you tell me what you did to Lyah. Is she alive? What are you going to do to her?” Keith’s eyes widened, having no control of his mouth. Where had that come from? Keith had half a mind to slap himself.

Charlie smiled, though it was more calculating than anything. “You’ve got balls. I’ll give you that. I suppose it doesn’t hurt to tell you.” Charlie started pacing. “Lyah, as I’ve come to learn her name, made a big mistake stealing from me. If I wasn’t caught off guard that night, I would’ve shot her for even being in my pockets. But alas, she caught me on a night of leisure, a night I decided to forget my business, my mind elsewhere.

“She destroyed my drugs, left me hanging in more ways than I’d like to admit. So, for dragging me across the country, I’m going to make her suffer. And suffer she will, tonight. When I’m done with her, she’s going to wish she had it easy like Presley.”

Who the hell was Presley? Charlie read the question in his eyes. “Lyah had me going for a while. I thought she was part of a rival gang trying to take what wasn’t theirs, and so I took him out. Turns out, Lyah was in a world all her own. She will pay for that, too. Presley was like a brother to me once. But I learned cousins should stay cousins.”

Keith tried to process all the information coming at him. So, she was still alive, but by the way Charlie was speaking, not for long. Charlie stopped pacing and held out his hand, the amusement dancing in his eyes from telling his story, long gone. "Now, less questions and more giving."

Reluctantly, Keith pulled out the cash from his pockets and handed it to him. Charlie smelled the stack and smirked. "Smells like interest to me. I like you, Keith. Despite you nearly giving me a concussion the night we met, you're not so bad. And because you came through for your… whatever she is to you… I'm giving you a pass. You can walk away from here, no strings attached. I was there that night she tried to steal your car, and though you did harm me, I understand. She took advantage of you, too.

"Turn a blind eye. Walk away and leave this—and her—in your past, and I'll never bother you again. You have my word."

"And leave Lyah? Why can't you let her go? You got the money. More than you asked," Keith found himself saying.

Charlie fixed a glare at Lyah's still body. "Lyah and I have some unfinished business. You need not worry about her. She's caused you more trouble than she's worth. You best be on your way unless you'd like a spot next to her. I've got plenty of rounds in my chamber."

Keith jumped at the sound of a gun cocking and realized the bald guy had brandished a handgun from his waistband. Keith gulped. He couldn't leave Lyah like this, not after everything they'd been through. But what choice did he have? He wanted to live, to see his family again. There was an easy way out the door, and he could go home and pretend nothing happened. No one would even know who Lyah was.

Keith took one last look at Lyah and turned to Charlie. Tears threatened to spill from his eyes as he said, "I'll leave, and I won't look back."

Charlie smiled and nodded. "Smart kid. I'll even through you a bone. I won't let my men follow you out the door. But know that once you leave through that door, you are no longer allowed back in."

Keith looked at the men's faces; their stone-cold glares all centered on him. Keith nodded and backed away further and further until his backside hit the door. With a tear running down his face, he whispered, "I'm sorry, Lyah."

He turned and walked out.

Chapter Eighteen

Lyah

Lyah's mouth tasted of stale beer and bad breath. She struggled to open her eyes as a warm light centered on her face. Her head was pounding, and her senses foggy, but she could make out the faint conversation around her. Her limbs felt like heavyweights.

Where was she? The events of earlier came flooding back to her in a rush and she felt her heart palpitations rise. She hadn't moved a muscle yet, though judging by the binding on her arms and legs, it would be futile. She had hoped this was all a dream.

Karma had finally caught up with her.

Lyah suppressed a moan as she blinked, once, twice, then settled on squinting. The light was so bright it was making her headache feel worse. Finally, her breathing calmed, and she did her best to figure out where she was as discretely as possible.

The floor she was on was smooth but dusty. It reminded her of a theater stage she'd used to dance on in her youth. Wait, theater? Had she been brought to the theater she was supposed to meet Charlie?

A flash of his smile in the truck slammed into her, and she realized the dire situation she was in. They had brought her to the theater and tied her up on stage. But why? Was there an audience? What was he planning?

She could hear a door open and close. She couldn't turn to see who was there with her position on the floor, but she could hear the conversation echoing around her.

"Nice of you to finally join us," Charlie said. Who was he speaking to? "Miss me? I believe you have something for me?"

Was the question directed to her? Had he found out she was awake?

The voice she heard next almost caused her to react. "Not until you tell me what you did to Lyah. Is she alive? What are you going to do to her?"

What was Keith doing here? Did he get the money at the casino? Was he captured, too? Or did he come to rescue her?

As sweet as that gesture may be, he was in more danger because of her. He should've run when he had the chance.

She decided to listen. Maybe she'd get the answers without having to move a muscle. In the meantime, she needed a plan to escape. But with the bindings on her wrist and legs, she'd have to find ways with her eyes and use her head.

"You've got balls. I'll give you that. I suppose it doesn't hurt to tell you," Charlie replied. Lyah slowly moved her head on the floor, trying to see if there was a place she could scoot toward, but the stage was empty in her peripheral. She'd have to get behind the red curtains in the corners of the stage in order to get away. But with her being front and center, they'd catch any movement she'd make.

Charlie proceeded to launch into his story, "Lyah, as I've come to learn her name, made a big mistake stealing from me. If I wasn't caught off guard that night, I would've shot her for even being in my pockets."

And yet, it took him forever to find her. Charlie played a big game, but could he aim? Lyah wanted to let out a snarky comment, but she remembered where she was and her predicament. Now was the wrong time and place to taunt a deranged man looking for any excuse to exact his revenge.

"But alas, she caught me on a night of leisure, a night I decided to forget my business, my mind elsewhere. She destroyed my drugs, left me hanging in more ways than I'd like to admit. So, for dragging me across the country, I'm going to make her suffer. And suffer she will, tonight. When I'm done with her, she's going to wish she had it easy like Presley."

Presley… she heard that name before. Maybe at the motel? Did Charlie kill him because of her? The idea of her being responsible for someone else's ill fate made her stomach twist. She almost bulked with vomit.

If she wasn't careful, she'd end up like Presley, whatever happened to him. Charlie was preparing her for something, and she didn't want to find out.

Charlie continued, "Lyah had me going for a while. I thought she was part of a rival gang trying to take what wasn't theirs, and so I took him out. Turns out, Lyah was in a world all her own. She will pay for that, too. Presley was like a brother to me once. But I learned cousins should stay cousins."

Cousin? If he was willing to off his own cousin off an assumption, there's no telling what he would do to her.

There were movements and some more talking, but Lyah tried to stay focused on her area. She could slightly spy the top of Charlie's head and four others standing in the rows in front of the stage. The place was otherwise empty from where she could see. With the tiniest shift, she tried to scoot to the wall but stopped when one of Charlie's men began to study her.

She stiffened and closed her eyes for a moment, then peeked to see if he was still looking. Thankfully, he had turned away.

"Turn a blind eye. Walk away and leave this—and her—in your past, and I'll never bother you again. You have my word."

Lyah held her breath. She couldn't believe what she was hearing. Charlie was going to let him walk? A dreaded feeling descended on her, whether at the prospect of Keith leaving her in the hands of a killer or knowing she would never see him again, she wasn't sure.

But Lyah didn't want Keith to pay for the mistakes she made. He deserved his happy ending, even at the expense of Lyah never finding hers. And so, she silently prayed Keith would turn his back to her and walk away. She wouldn't hate him. She never could. She'd hate herself more if something happened to him.

"And leave Lyah? Why can't you let her go? You got the money. More than you asked." Why couldn't Keith just leave? Charlie got what he wanted, and he wouldn't hand over Lyah, not after everything she'd done. There was no point in asking.

Lyah tilted her head slightly to see if she could get a better look at the men in the audience. The two that threw her into the truck were standing with their arms folded in the aisle while the driver and bald man who followed her were closer to Charlie. Craning her neck more, the air left her lungs when she caught Charlie's glare. Quickly, she closed her eyes, praying he hadn't seen her looking.

"Lyah and I have some unfinished business. You need not worry about her. She's caused you more trouble than she's worth. You best be on your way unless you'd like a spot next to her. I've got plenty of rounds in my chamber."

She pleaded for Keith to heed his words. By the look on Charlie's face, they were not empty threats. He was done playing. Done being taken advantage of.

As if on cue, she heard a gun cock. Startled, she opened her eyes again, but this time, she was able to find Keith standing near the entrance, his gaze on her. Whether he could see her face, she wasn't sure, but his next words caused the back of her eyes to sting. "I'll leave, and I won't look back."

Lyah inhaled and shuttered a breath as a few tears slipped onto the stage floor. He was making the right choice. She had to believe that even if her heart was screaming otherwise. Her mind drifted to all the memories they made on the road together and all the laughter and frustration they shared. It was truly the best memories she would cherish for a lifetime.

She didn't hear what Charlie said next. The only thing that registered was the opening and closing of a door and then silence. Lyah sent a spiritual goodbye to Keith and let the tears flow onto the stage floor.

It was time to face the music.

"I know you're awake. There's no sense in hiding it." Instead of answering, Lyah laid still, allowing Charlie to walk on stage and stand next to her. He crouched down and stared at the pool of tears next to her face, her vision glassy and her breathing constricted from the stuffy nose. "You brought this on yourself. These tears mean nothing to me."

"They aren't for you," she spat, though the lack of use of her voice for a time made it scratchy and less vindictive.

Charlie craned his neck and assessed her. "Well, he's not coming back. In fact," Charlie stood up and spread his arms facing the four-man audience, "no one is coming to save you. How does that make you feel, hmm? Being left with nothing but the clothes on your back? Do you really think crying will get you out of this? Those tears are wasted on a coward. Save it for real pain like this!"

Charlie turned and kicked her hard in her stomach, the wind getting knocked from her lungs. Her eyes stung, and she wheezed as the tip of his hard boot sunk into her belly two more times. She struggled to cough as she curled into herself, unable to clutch her stomach like she wanted to.

Charlie circled her, hands behind his back as he spoke again. "My original plan was to shoot you right away. Maybe from afar or have one of my men take you out. But I much prefer this way. Up close and personal. A warm welcome from me to you."

He stopped in front of her again and stooped once more. "I can't wait to watch you bleed." He grabbed her by her brown locks and pulled her head up, only to slam her head back onto the stage floor, which only served to intensify her headache. The left side of her jaw began to seer with pain, and the roots of her hair felt as it was breaking skin from how tight he still held her. Stars threatened to dance in front of her eyes.

"I want to watch you suffer for putting me through so much. Losing my money, losing my drugs, giving me blue balls, taking out my cousin, following you across the country. So much trouble you caused me because you wanted to have sticky fingers. Well, now it's my time to show you how I like to play when I'm not drunk. You're going to put on a nice show for me."

He released her hair and let her drop to the floor. He walked off the stage and into the audience. Her eyes now wide open, she watched as he took something from the bald man and held it up to her.

A gun.

Lyah did her best to sit up and face him. If he was going to shoot her, she might as well ask some questions before it was too late. Some dots needed connecting. "How did you keep finding us?"

Charlie chuckled; the gun still raised. She couldn't see his facial expression clearly with the light in her eyes, but the gun was enough to keep track of. "More questions? You can't talk your way out of this one."

Lyah breath stuttered as she fought to keep her position. The way her legs were tied made it difficult to sit up, not to mention a mounting pain was in her stomach. The bastard had kicked right in her old wound. "Just tell me before you shoot me. It's the least you can do."

"I don't like taking orders. But since you won't live to see outside these walls, I guess I can offer an answer. Having the right connections gives you the right tools. That shot that you heard hit the back of the car wasn't a bullet."

The answer caught her off guard. "What?"

Charlie inched closer to the stage. "That's right. Black market GPS bullet tracker. A gift from an ex-cop."

The bald man stepped forward as if introducing himself, his hands clasped in front of him. He stood like a military man waiting for a signal from his captain. If Charlie had an ex-cop on his payroll, there's no telling what he could do. What kind of power did he hold?

Charlie continued. "Not to mention, the homeless old man at the gas station the two of you stopped at had plenty to say about your lack of monetary generosity. He told us everything he heard."

That old bastard.

"After he—" Charlie pointed to the ex-cop "—ran you two off the road, it was easy to have my other men follow your every move. Where one failed, the other picked up. You were never too far from them. Maybe from me as I was a few states away. But they kept every eye on you two."

Lyah's judgment that night was way off. Of all the people she could piss off, she just had to pick this guy. "Were you ever planning on letting me go? Why give me a meeting time and spot if you were going to kidnap me anyway?"

"Consider it a security measure. I wanted to give you the benefit of the doubt, but ultimately, if I couldn't trust you to have two thousand bucks in your vicinity, why should I trust you with twenty? You've already spent nearly half of what you stole."

Lyah hadn't even thought about the money she initially took from him. Her pockets had lessened in weight.

"Turns out, the Princeton nerd was more reliable than you. Now, if you're done wasting time, I'd like to have a little fun."

The lights suddenly went out, leaving the entire room in complete blackness. Lyah was quick to throw herself into action and scoot as fast as she could to the other side of the stage. Cursing and shuffling footsteps could be heard running onto the stairs by the stage. Panic started to set in as a shot rang out. A blistering pain in her left thigh caused her to scream out.

The sound of several heavy objects hitting the stage floor around her forced her to continue where her memory served her right. A few groans were heard, and Charlie yelled, "Stop being a klutz and secure her!" much closer than she liked.

Lyah couldn't see a thing, so when someone grabbed her from behind and began dragging her across the stage, she squirmed against her attacker to free herself, which only caused her more pain. Screaming would draw more of them in her direction, and so she chose to keep quiet. It was only when she felt the floor lower did she realize what was going on. It was a stage lift.

"I got you. Just stay quiet until we reach the bottom," Keith whispered in her ear.

He came back for her!

Tears sprang from her eyes as she leaned into him as the floor came to a stop. It was still a little dark wherever they were, but Keith took charge to undo her hands and feet.

He gasped when he felt blood on his fingers.

They had no time to stop. "We need to get going! If they fall through the floor here, we're doomed. Just pick me up and run!" Lyah whispered. She couldn't see him completely, but she imagined he nodded. He did as she said and cradled her into his arms, then quietly hurried from the area.

There was a door nearby that Keith tried but failed to open as he carried her. He tried two others and also could not open them.

"There's a stage lift right here!" They heard someone shout.

Keith froze for a moment then hurried down the hall.

"Do you know your way out? How did you get back in?"

Slightly out of breath, Keith replied, "I never left. I thought about it, and I realized friends don't leave friends behind. So, I worked out a quick plan to get you away. Turns out, turning off the lights was all I really needed to do, though I couldn't save you from getting hurt. I'm sorry."

He didn't leave her after all. She was elated to hear that, but their predicament stopped her from rejoicing.

Blood was pooling from Keith's hands holding her legs, but the initial pain hurt worse than it did now, though it was still excruciating. She did her best to put her mind off it until they were safe enough to assess. For now, she'd have to bear through with gritted teeth.

Keith rushed down the hall until they finally came upon a red exit sign over a door. Without a hitch, he ran straight through it and onto the wet pavement outside.

They made it out, but they were far from being in the clear. The lingering smell of rain still permeated the air though the skies were slowly clearing. Keith ran behind the truck parked not too far and placed Lyah down on the ground. With her leg accumulating blood rapidly, he tore a piece of his shirt and used one of the ropes from her hands to secure the fabric over the wound. Lyah hissed with pain as he knotted it and tried to get her to stand. The material was thin and would soak through soon, but it was better than leaving it open for infection.

"Can you stand?"

Lyah tried but hissed again and lifted her injured leg. Without help, she wouldn't get very far on her own.

Keith wrapped her arm around his shoulder to take some pressure off her leg. "Just hold on to me as much as possible."

"How are we going to get out of here? We'd have to walk across the empty parking lot to get to the other side, but they'd see us, and they're likely already close."

Keith looked back at the door they had just busted through, then turned to her. "We improvise until the cops get here."

Lyah's eyes widened. "You called them? When? How?"

"This building isn't abandoned like I thought; otherwise, the lights wouldn't have worked. Turns out, there's still a phone line at the ticket booth. I called them about a hostage situation at the theater before I came to you. They should be here any minute."

If she could kiss him, she would.

"Keith… thank you—"

"Don't thank me yet. We still have to stall Charlie and his men. Who knows how long it'll take for the cops to get here? We're going to need a story, too."

Lyah was done running. "How about the truth?"

Keith's eyes softened when he looked at her. She didn't get time to analyze it though because five men burst through the door they had gone through moments before.

Still behind the truck, Keith held her close as the men fanned out, a gun in Charlie's hand as they looked around. "Come out, come out, wherever you are! You can't hide from me for long, Lyah. I will always find you."

The men who snatched Lyah the first time cornered the truck as they surrounded them from either side. It was pointless to hide. Lyah yelled out, "If you promise not to hurt him, we'll come out!"

"Lyah!" Keith exclaimed with anger.

Lyah touched his cheek and said, "There's no point in trying to save me, Keith. I appreciate the gesture, I do. But my number is up."

"But the cops—"

"Aren't here yet and probably won't be by the time he decides to send off a shot."

Charlie yelled, "I promise you nothing! Was this all part of your plan? It was rather flawed if it was."

The two men descended upon them, grabbing them both and ripping them apart. Lyah fell against the dark-skinned man then onto the ground. Her injured leg was not able to bear the weight of her body. Keith struggled against the other guy as he was brought to Charlie. Lyah was picked up by her arm and dragged beside Keith. She could barely stand, but she had no other choice.

Charlie tapped the gun against his chin. "Hmm, it seems it was all just a show. An elaborate scheme between two liars and thieves." Charlie focused his attention on Keith. "I should've tied you up next to your girlfriend. That's twice now you two have taken advantage of my kindness. This will be your last."

He pointed the gun to Keith's face, and a scream escaped Lyah's lips. "No! Don't hurt him, please! I'm the one you want!"

"Lyah, no!"

Charlie lifted a brow. "Oh? And yet you played me for a fool more than once. I can't allow that. I don't like embarrassment. But since you asked so kindly, I'll let you go first, and then your boyfriend can join you at the gates of hell."

The gun swung to her, and a bang echoed through her ears. Before she knew it, she fell to the ground. Her heart was pounding a million miles a minute, and her skin began to radiate heat as if she had really fallen to the pits of hell. Her stomach felt like a gaping hole was inside it. Like it was ripping from the inside out.

She almost didn't register Keith's scream, and the sirens in the background nor the shoveling of feet as Charlie and his men packed into the black truck and sped out off the lot as several police cars pulled up. Another zipped past after the truck in pursuit.

It all happened so fast.

Suddenly, Keith was in front of her as he cradled her body, her limbs flimsy, lacking motor. "Why would you do that, Lyah? We were so close. So close…"

"Do you regret it? Any of it?" she asked as she choked on blood.

Lyah sure did. There was so much she regretted, more in the last week than in her entire life. She regretted dragging Keith into her mess instead of meeting him under friendly circumstances because he was a great guy after all. She regretted leaving like a coward the night before instead of making their last night special.

"Never. You gave me something I couldn't get from anyone else."

She briefly registered a police officer pulling Keith away from her and asking if he was okay. Two others came over and accessed her wounds, pulling, prodding, and talking over her haze.

Every sound seemed muffled, the air had become still, and Lyah's muscles started to relax. And though her entire body had become a canvas of numbness and burning, she wondered at the peaceful feeling that had overcome her.

It was almost majestic the way she could feel her heartbeat bouncing through her body. It felt so powerful and lively. If she didn't have the grasp of her life slipping away little-by-little, she might've been amazed by how serene she felt and how panicked her body had become. This feeling was foreign but welcoming.

"Miss! Stay with me! Keep your eyes open!"

So tired. Her lids began to slip. She wanted to sleep. The feeling was creeping on her. It felt so peaceful.

Finally, it felt like her body had caught up with her mind. Her heart rate slowed, and she could feel her fingers uncurl from her fist.

"Lyah! Open your eyes, dammit! You're not leaving me! Not now." Keith's shouting became faint, and his face started to blur. She looked over at him being pulled away by a cop so the others could stay medically attentive to her body. The tears running down his face almost tore her apart. It wasn't until she felt something wet touch her ears that she realized she was crying, too.

She wanted to tell him to let go. That she would be fine. She didn't want to hold him back any longer. But the words died on her lips as she slipped further away.

It was strange knowing someone cared for her and valued her life. Acknowledging it, unlike how she'd ignored James' attempts to show her worth. Would Keith miss her if she were to go? Would he remember her and all the fun they had? Lyah certainly would. After all, it was the only time in her life she'd felt real companionship. The only time she welcomed it.

She would hold tight those memories of their week together until they met again. Whenever or wherever that would be. But even with all the wrong that happened and all she regretted, Lyah wouldn't change a single thing if that meant she would meet Keith all over again.

Epilogue

Keith

One year later

"Geez! How much stuff did you pack?" Mick asked as he tried to stuff the last suitcase into the trunk of Keith's car.

"Do you have to complain every time you put something in the car? Hurry up so we can go before Mom and Dad change their mind about you coming." Keith rounded his new black Toyota Corolla to start it up.

The air was stifling, and he needed air conditioning like no tomorrow. Mick finished up what he was doing in the trunk and sat in the passenger seat with a gleeful smile directed toward his older brother. "I can't believe they agreed to this."

"Don't jinx it. They might catch wind of your excitement and cancel the trip."

"They wouldn't do that!"

"Then, you don't know Mom and Dad."

It wasn't easy to convince their parents to let Mick tag along on a cross-country road trip to California as a graduation present to Mick. Like Keith, Mick had spent most of his life sheltered in their parents' shadow. He was a grade-A student, stuck to his studies and school activities, but had trouble understanding their parents' lifestyle and lashed out often.

In their small family, Mick was often seen as the rebellious one for being so outspoken. He never disrespected their parents, but he found himself at odds with them more often. That was why Keith wanted to give him a break from their parents and embark on a cross-country trip to San Francisco to enjoy the westside beaches for a few weeks.

Mick turned on the music and jammed out to an old hip-hop song while Keith tried to follow the GPS from his phone as they cruised down the road. He had forgotten to get a magnetic stand for it when he was shopping for their trip. Keith made a mental note to find one at their first stop since he struggled to keep the phone propped on the dashboard with his makeshift stand.

"Do you want me to hold the phone and point the directions for you? You look stressed."

His brother was a lifesaver, and he didn't even know it. "Please."

Mick took his phone and pointed out the directions with ease. Keith felt more relaxed without the pressure of multitasking. Soon, he was bopping his head along to the music alongside his brother. It wasn't his preferred tune, but he was more open-minded than he was a year ago.

Epilogue

It had been such a long time since he was able to feel at ease on the road. After returning from Las Vegas, he refused to drive or look at another car. It wasn't that he was afraid to be on the road, but the memories tormented him.

Mick directed him onto the highway, and for the next couple hours, they talked and enjoyed each other's company like they hadn't before. Growing up, they weren't exactly close, something Keith wished he could go back and change. Mick was a cool guy to be around, and they had a lot more in common than he realized.

Keith was hellbent on leaving the house once he reached eighteen. By that time, Mick was barely in high school and had found his own clique. They never got fully acquainted as adults. Now that Mick was eighteen, Keith thought it was about time they spend some quality brother time together. After all, life couldn't be taken for granted, Keith learned.

They were on the topic of cars when Mick asked, "Whatever happened to that old piece of junk Dad gave you?"

"You mean the wagon?"

"Yeah. You never did tell me where it went. You left with it but came back without it. What's up with that?"

What was his excuse again? Something about running off the road and the wagon getting totaled. Technically, it wasn't a lie though many details were omitted. He had to get more creative with his excuse to his parents, the police, and the insurance company when he finally got around to calling them about the abandoned car in the forest. His father was furious but unexpectedly expressed he was grateful for his safety. They bought his story about catching a ride to Las Vegas, and he was able to get a new car through his insurance company.

He could've told the truth if he wanted. It would've been easier, but Keith wanted to respect Lyah's lifestyle and her choices that led them to their unfortunate end. But he also didn't want to share her memory with his parents. They didn't deserve her story.

The lies rolled off his tongue like he was born to do it, and it strangely brought a sense of peace to him, knowing he was channeling her in some ways. She had taught him bad habits, but he was grateful to her for showing him the world.

Lyah.

Even now, that name sent a shiver down his spine. That last night at the theater… He shook his head, refocusing on the road. If he got distracted now, there was no telling what he'd do.

It wasn't until Mick snapped his fingers in front of his face that he realized he never answered Mick's question.

"Damn, where did you go?"

"Huh?" Keith blinked.

"You just started staring off ahead like you were somewhere else. Did you hear anything I said?"

Had Mick been talking the whole time?

Mick rolled his eyes and turned to his window. "Whatever. Forget it."

Keith opened his mouth then closed it, unsure what to say. He promised himself he wasn't going down that path–down memory lane. But it was inevitable. They flooded his mind like he was with her only yesterday.

Stepping off that plane after everything went down with Lyah, Keith barely spoke about the situation beyond what he had to for the police report. His parents and friends worried about his sudden change in attitude and lack of interest in anything but staring off into space for hours. Never did he utter her name in their presence. Lyah was like a bad and good dream that he only wanted to share with himself. A part of him only wanted her to stay alive in his memories because it meant that what they shared on their journey was only for him. It was special to him; he realized.

But sitting with his younger brother in the car and seeing Mick trying to connect with him, Keith suddenly felt the urge to share those memories.

"You promise not to tell?"

Mick turned to him, confused. "Not to tell what?"

"The real story. I'll tell you what really happened, but you have to promise not to tell anyone. Especially Mom and Dad."

"You don't even have to ask. You have my word."

Keith knew he could always trust Mick. If there was one thing Mick took seriously was loyalty. He admired him for that.

Keith wondered where to begin. There were many layers to the story. He wasn't even sure he could explain it right. But ultimately, he decided to start with what Mick knew of his plans to stop Tally's wedding.

He detailed finding out about Tally's Las Vegas rendezvous and setting out on what was supposed to be a romantic journey to express his love for a girl he thought he'd lost. He talked about first meeting Lyah, how much trouble they had gotten into with Charlie, and how running for their life turned into a trip he'd never forget.

Keith reminisced on the aggravation of taking care of Lyah and having her tag along on his journey. But a pleasant smile penetrated his features as he remembered the fun they had and how much he learned from her.

He shared their late-night talks, her willingness to help him even after the mean things he said to her or thought of her. It had seemed life knocked her down at every turn, but she still found ways to stand on her own.

Keith noted just how strong she was even in the presence of danger. She taught him about courage.

As he drew their adventure story to a close, the grip he held on the steering wheel turned his knuckles white. The questions on Mick's face were notable, and Keith braced himself for a barrage of them.

"Wow. If I didn't know you, I'd think you were retelling a story you read. I can't believe you were on the run. Who would've thought? And this Lyah girl, where is she now? Did she go to the hospital? Is she…?"

How could he answer when he didn't know much himself? After she passed out, Keith finally removed himself from the cop's embrace and sat by Lyah's side as the ambulance had arrived to take her.

"Sir, I need to take her into the ambulance. Can you let go, please?"

The paramedic was so calm it would've pissed him off if he wasn't about to fall apart. He wanted the world to feel as angry and sad as he felt at the moment. Eventually, he had no choice but to let her go as several paramedics surrounded her to take vitals and hook her up to oxygen. She had passed out just before the ambulance arrived. Her limps hung as they placed her on the stretcher.

Keith stood with shaky hands, his clothes stained with Lyah's blood. He was confused as to what to do next. The paramedics tried to ask him some questions about his health, but he was in shock and couldn't form an answer. At some point, they sat him down on the edge of another ambulance he had no idea was there and offered him a bottle of water and a thin blanket.

But he couldn't drink, nor could he think. He wanted to be near Lyah. The door closed to the ambulance, and he shot up from his seat, the blanket from around his shoulders falling gracefully to the wet pavement.

"I want to ride with her. Please!"

A paramedic came over to him and placed a hand on his chest to sit him down. "Sir, I can't let you do that. She's lost a lot of blood, and they're working on her as we speak. Plus, you're in shock, and we need to ask you some questions as well as the police."

No! He needed to leave! He needed to see her. The ambulance carrying her switched on their sirens and pulled out from the curbside, distancing itself from him.

"I need to be by her side! Please!" Keith pleaded.

The paramedic looked behind him, and a police officer with a small notebook in hand came into view. The officer took in Keith's appearance, and with a sympathetic sigh, he nodded toward the other ambulance truck.

"It's in your best interest to hop into the ambulance and get a checkup, son. I'll ask you questions once the doctors give us the okay. For now, the other officers will secure the scene." With a pat on the shoulder, the officer made his way back to his cruiser.

The paramedic took his arm gently and led him to the front of the truck. "Are you sure you're not hurt anywhere? I'll let you sit up front, but it'll likely be a bumpy ride."

Keith was so worried about Lyah, he hadn't checked to see if he was physically injured. He felt mostly numb, but that didn't mean he wasn't hurt. Keith ultimately shook his head and was escorted to the passenger side of the ambulance. Another paramedic was talking to the officer but disappeared at the ambulance's back when he saw them.

The ride to the hospital was silent and long. Keith was anxious to know what was going on with Lyah. It was hard to wrap his mind around the worst-case scenario. How dire was her situation?

She lost a lot of blood, and the bullet was likely still embedded in her wound. Also, she never fully healed from the car accident and was shot in the leg.

By the time they made it to the hospital, Keith nearly chewed off his fingers. The anxiety he felt would last longer than he hoped as he was whisked away by doctors and held for a few hours. He was asked about his physicality and his mental state. Eventually, doctors came to their own conclusions and released him to the officer waiting outside his room. It was the same one from the theater.

Keith tried to find out what was going on with Lyah, but little information was given. The officer only knew that she was in surgery. Instead, Keith was bombarded with questions about the incident.

"What did you tell him? Did you lie?" Mick asked, his gaze intrigued on his side profile as Keith lost himself to the yellow lines in the road.

"No, not really. I left out the part about Lyah stealing from Charlie even though there was no evidence of her crime. It was dirty money anyway. I was nervous, though. How do you convey a story like ours enough for them to catch the guy without incriminating both of us and letting Mom and Dad find out?"

"Well, whatever you said worked," Mick pointed out.

It did, but Keith worried that protecting them would hinder justice. Not to mention, they had a hand in Charlie's violent backlash. From the money to the brick and the running—they both had a hand in it. It was a mess from the start.

"Do you know the guy who shot your friend?" the officer, Martinez, asked.

"No, not really."

Officer Martinez quirked an eyebrow, his pen hovering over the notepad. "I'm gonna need you to specify for me. Do you know the assailant?"

"I know his name is Charlie."

He resumed writing, "How do you know Charlie?"

"We met at a motel in Pennsylvania, where I also met Lyah."

Officer Martinez stopped writing. "Pennsylvania?"

Keith nodded. "He followed her here."

"What business did Charlie and Lyah have together?"

Keith opened his mouth and closed it, not sure what to say. He needed to protect him and Lyah, but he also wanted the guy caught. "Charlie was... Charlie was her date from a bar."

"She told you this?"

"Yes, she did."

Officer Martinez wrote that down. "How did you and Lyah end up running from Charlie across state lines?"

Keith went on to tell Officer Martinez how Lyah had refused sexual advances from Charlie and ran into Keith on her way out of the motel, only for them to end up running from Charlie because he was waving a gun and accusing Keith of being in cahoots with Lyah. He expressed that she was afraid that Charlie would find her if she called the police because of his connections and how their belongings had eventually been stolen and damaged.

The story rolled off his tongue like liquid. Keith liked to think Lyah would be proud of him for covering their behind while still maintaining some truth. He debated about telling Officer Martinez about Presley. He couldn't confirm or deny Charlie's story, and as bad he felt about it, Keith decided to keep his mouth shut. Charlie would get what was coming to him. He was sure of that.

After a few more questions, Officer Martinez handed him a card stating to call if anything else happened and that the other officers were still chasing Charlie and his men. Keith made sure to note Charlie was likely in a gang or a drug dealer or both.

Once Officer Martinez left, Keith didn't waste any time looking for Lyah's room.

"Did you ever find her?"

Keith nodded. "Yeah. By the time I found her room, she was out of surgery. I had to make up a lie to the doctor to get information. I was able to see her for only a few minutes before they told me she couldn't have visitors."

Truthfully, he had lied and said he was her fiancé for the doctor to tell him it was touch and go. They had to take out the bullet from her wounds, and she lost a massive amount of blood. The bullet that had hit her stomach missed her vital organs by mere inches, and the one in her leg missed her femoral artery. She also had a concussion. But she was comatose, and there was no telling when or if she would wake.

It was heartbreaking getting that news and seeing her lay in the bed so still and on breathing machines. It made him want to break all over again. The girl lying in bed looked so beaten and fragile, so unlike the bright-eyed wildfire he'd come to befriend. So, he whispered in her ears to fight every moment he spent with her. She was unconscious for the duration of the time Keith was there—three whole days.

"Whatever happened to Charlie? Did they catch him?" Mick pointed to an exit Keith was supposed to take.

"They did, but not until I had already left for home. They lost him in the car chase but found his hideout. It turns out even without the incident, he was already wanted for several drug charges and warrants. Not to mention, they had evidence he was involved in Presley's murder. But since Lyah couldn't testify and I was out of state, several other witnesses sealed the case. He'll be in prison for the rest of his life."

"Aren't you scared of retaliation?"

At first, yes. The police never caught the bald guy from Charlie's group, and Keith spent months looking over his shoulder. But at some point, Keith got tired of living in fear and eventually decided if anyone were to come for him, then so be it. But nothing ever happened.

"Not anymore."

Mick didn't ask any more questions, leaving Keith to reminisce about the past year without Lyah. It was hard, but as much as the memories hindered him, they were also keeping him going.

It would take several days to get to San Francisco with several stops and sightseeing along the way. Keith enjoyed every moment of it, especially taking the same streets he and Lyah had taken on their journey. He would point out each area's significance to his stories, and Mick grew more and more empathetic with every tale.

It was like once he had opened his mouth, he couldn't help but talk about Lyah. Every memory was etched in his mind like a drawing. Like just yesterday, he was telling her how much she irritated him.

By the time they reached their beachside destination, his mouth had run tired, and he was ready to get his vacation on. Once situated in their hotel room, Mick flopped on the bed face first with a pleasant sigh.

"Ah! This is what I imagine heaven feels like."

The comforter was feathery and plush enough to call Keith under them. He reprimanded himself for dirtying the sheets with his travel clothes, but it was an experience he dared not pass up.

"I can smell the ocean from here," Mick said in a dreamy tone.

With the beach just outside their window five stories down, it was the perfect view and smell for vacation. Keith knew he made the right choice.

They slept for what felt like minutes and then decided to take advantage of the beach's hot sunny day by joining the crowds on the boardwalk nearby. They showered and changed and headed out to enjoy what was left of the afternoon before they would go to dinner.

"Do you plan on hooking up with any girls?" Mick asked, bumping shoulders with Keith playfully.

"Uh..."

"I'll take that as, 'I'm too shy, I'll let them come to me.'" Mick mocked. His brother knew him well. Picking up women was not something he was ever good at, and he was sure a trip to California would not change that fact.

They browsed the boardwalk, pointing out all the cool areas, and then decided to hop in line at an ice cream shop. The line was decent but slow-moving as only one man was taking and processing orders.

Keith took to surveying the boardwalk, noting how busy and lively the area was. "So, why couldn't Lyah testify anyway?"

Keith turned to his brother with a frown. "Huh?"

"You heard me. You never explained why Lyah couldn't testify against Charlie."

Keith opened his mouth to answer, but a familiar glint of curly brown hair caught his eye in the distance. Absentmindedly, he bypassed his brother's protest and maneuvered out of line to get a closer look as if drawn majestically to the sight.

A woman in a short blue jumpsuit stood far ahead of him, the crowd engulfing her presence. The physique was right, the hair was spot on.

Could it be?

He knew it was dumb to follow but pounded forward anyway, struggling to catch up. Finally, he approached the woman and gently grabbed her shoulder on impulse, spinning her around to face him.

"Lyah?" He visibly deflated as the unfamiliar woman frowned at him.

"I-I'm sorry. I thought you were someone else."

The woman *hmphed* and continued her way, eventually getting swallowed by the crowd. What was he thinking? It couldn't have been her.

Mick caught up with him sometime after and handed him his vanilla ice cream cone, though Keith didn't feel like eating it anymore. "What was all that about? You scared the poor woman away."

Keith shook his head. "It was nothing. I just… I thought... Never mind. Let's go."

Mick gave him a peculiar look but didn't argue. He continued trying to school him on the proper way to pick up women, but it fell on deaf ears.

As Keith finally managed to get an appetite, he looked up from his walk of shame to give attention to his melting cone when he came to a screeching halt, unbeknown to Mick, who kept walking and talking to himself.

Those eyes staring back at him. He hadn't seen them since she laid in his arms, bleeding out from a gunshot wound. Those were the brown tresses he was looking for earlier. And that smile, he was hoping to see again after leaving the hospital.

Lyah.

He called the hospital every day after he left, hoping for good news. The staff only ever related that information could only be released to family in person. Days after Charlie's conviction, he was told she had been released.

He spent days pondering about her condition, whether she would call or show up at his doorstep, even with the knowledge that she had no phone or had the slightest idea of where he lived. He wondered how her injuries were, if she had permanent damage or if she recovered fully like he hoped. Had she gone home with her mother, who came to the hospital the day he was released and barred him from visiting again after hearing about what happened?

Did she remember him at all?

He remembered her—every minute since the day he left the hospital. The letter she gave him—the one he always kept in his pocket—

was the only thing he had left of her.

Sitting on a bench outside the surf shop, her hair pulled back, her cheeks rosy, and that ever-present smile etched on her face as she gazed back at him. The sun was looking out for him today, and it shined right on her as if she were an angel.

Was she?

Either way, Keith could only stop and smile back, feeling like he finally found what he'd been searching for his whole life.

The End

Acknowledgments

I am grateful to all my readers and supporters. With COVID-19 breathing down all our necks, it has not been easy to write in the climate we are in, but I still rise.

Special thanks to my family for pushing me to complete this project through the crisis and for helping me keep my head up. Thank you to my beta readers and editors who were patient with me during my writing process.

I began this story shortly after Love Me Blind around 2010 and had come back to it on and off throughout the years. I wanted to write a completely different character from who I am personality-wise, which happened to be wildfire Lyah Artisan. I identified more with Keith, having planned out my life entirely only to be thrown curveballs all the time.

This was a good redemption story to me, and I wanted to show that even though someone may think they're alone in the world and have no one in their corner, they can get through anything. Lyah and Keith represented what I felt like in the years after high school—lost, alone, incapable of love, and indecisive. I'm sure many people have felt like that a time or two in their life.

This story was a lot of fun to write though I will admit that it wasn't easy to transition from writing romance to action scenes. I hope my readers at least enjoyed my attempt to make this story complete, and I look forward to pushing out more books in the future that dabble in action. To all my readers, please stay safe and be mindful of those around you. We can get through anything.

About the Author

Nandra Hoffman is a Canadian American who lives in sunny Florida with her family and pretends the hot weather keeps her pushing. Beaches and reading have become the joys of life and where her inspiration continues to hit. In 2019, she completed her bachelor's degree in Communications at Walden University. Her first book, Love Me Blind, was released on February 7, 2020, and is currently available on most platforms. She spends her days with her adorable husky, Dakota, and loves helping others with all their writing needs.

www.ingramcontent.com/pod-product-compliance
Lightning Source LLC
Chambersburg PA
CBHW021247200726
48288CB00015B/2570

* 9 7 8 1 9 5 0 6 9 7 0 9 0 *